To Janet,

Rhoda's favourite daughter!

Love and best wishes,

Thomas !

# *Smiling*
## THE
# MOON

D1350419

# Smiling
## THE
# MOON

## THOMAS LAWRENCE

**HAY HOUSE**

Carlsbad, California • New York City • London • Sydney
Johannesburg • Vancouver • Hong Kong • New Delhi

First published and distributed in the United Kingdom by:
Hay House UK Ltd, Astley House, 33 Notting Hill Gate, London W11 3JQ
Tel: +44 (0)20 3675 2450; Fax: +44 (0)20 3675 2451
www.hayhouse.co.uk

Published and distributed in the United States of America by:
Hay House Inc., PO Box 5100, Carlsbad, CA 92018-5100
Tel: (1) 760 431 7695 or (800) 654 5126
Fax: (1) 760 431 6948 or (800) 650 5115
www.hayhouse.com

Published and distributed in Australia by:
Hay House Australia Ltd, 18/36 Ralph St, Alexandria NSW 2015
Tel: (61) 2 9669 4299; Fax: (61) 2 9669 4144
www.hayhouse.com.au

Published and distributed in the Republic of South Africa by:
Hay House SA (Pty) Ltd, PO Box 990, Witkoppen 2068
Tel/Fax: (27) 11 467 8904
www.hayhouse.co.za

Published and distributed in India by:
Hay House Publishers India, Muskaan Complex, Plot No.3, B-2,
Vasant Kunj, New Delhi 110 070
Tel: (91) 11 4176 1620; Fax: (91) 11 4176 1630
www.hayhouse.co.in

Distributed in Canada by:
Raincoast, 9050 Shaughnessy St, Vancouver BC V6P 6E5
Tel: (1) 604 323 7100; Fax: (1) 604 323 2600

Text © Thomas Lawrence, 2013

This book is a work of fiction. The use of actual events or locales, and persons living or deceased, is strictly for artistic/literary reasons only.

The moral rights of the author have been asserted.

A catalogue record for this book is available from the British Library.

ISBN: 978-1-78180-171-0

Printed and bound in Great Britain by TJ International Ltd.

*For Maria*

*Gnoseer:* mystic, shaman; wise man or woman, steeped in the knowledge of the invisible realms, divining energy for the purpose of healing and altering events, seeing and knowing what most cannot. Origin: *gnosis/seer:* 'no-seer'/.

N
W
E
S
Kirndachan
Toprig
Brennan
North Highlands
Tulkney
Woulin
Tagoran
Traig
Mirney
Ballamar

Athale

Black Lake
• Kellin

• Teksol

Vik    corthairn

TULRAIN BASIN

• Aforan

Zugan •

• Kuik

South
Highlands

• Ballakuik

• Gallantore

ISLAND of BRACKA

# Chapter 1

*The sun always shines in your heart,*
*just be there and see.*

It was the fear in the boy's eyes that caught his attention. It was a look that bonded them seamlessly in time. It was a look he would never forget.

Wode was on the drover's road, enjoying the feeling of space – wide horizons – and the late sun warm on his face. Revelling in solitude, he'd been walking most of the day, allowing destiny to decide his journey. He'd set an easy pace that he could keep up from dawn till dusk, his long strides swallowing the miles. He was just passing the farm when the boy rounded the corner of the barn, legs pumping at top speed, looking over his shoulder, wary of pursuit. Their eyes met a fraction before he ran straight into Wode, ricocheted off and fell back hard to the ground. Wode stared down at the sprawled boy who sat momentarily stunned; through his surprise he could hear shouts. Still dazed, the boy got shakily to his feet. In his right hand, unbroken, was a fresh hen's egg gleaming white in the afternoon sun. Wode immediately sensed the situation and with unseen speed grabbed the boy's arm just as he began to take off.

"What are you doing?" cried the boy as he pulled at Wode's grip, panic rising.

"What are *you* doing?" replied Wode flatly.

"Let go, you...you!"

There was a brief struggle but the boy was no match for the vice-like grip of Wode, who stood tall and unmoved, coolly looking down at the wriggling mass of skinny arms and legs trying to wrench free.

They were joined by a puffing, thick-set man, who glowered down at the boy. "You little thief!" And then looking at Wode, "Thank you for catching this thieving leggit."

"You're welcome. Stealing eggs, is he?"

The man shot the boy a glance. "Aye. Little tyke."

Wode took in the mud-stained clothes and furious face glaring up at him. "What's your name, boy?"

"Jerreb."

Wode didn't believe him for a minute but he continued, "What are you up to?"

"None of your business," the boy shouted and stood there panting, taking an unusual interest in the ground at his feet. The farmer took a sharp intake of breath in frustration and was about to shout at him but stopped when Wode raised his hand. Wode waited for almost half a minute before repeating his question.

The boy was silent in his ebbing defiance and Wode saw the bravado drain out of him. A shadow passed across his eyes as he visibly slumped like a caged animal resigned to its stolen freedom. "You've not been doing this very long, have you?" Wode said more gently.

"How do you know?" the egg's cross owner enquired.

"Because he's not testing my grip and looking for a way out. And because he told me."

"What are you talking about? He's said nothing."

Wode turned and looked directly at the farmer. "His eyes, my friend. His eyes told me."

The farmer wasn't used to such a piercing look, he was more used to the benign, timeless gaze of his cattle and sheep. He felt a prickle of unease, as though his very soul was being examined. Wode saw it and smiled reassuringly at him.

"Well anyway," the farmer said huffily, turning back to the boy, "I want my egg back."

Wode gestured to the boy, who flashed him a brief look of resistance before he grudgingly obeyed, dropping his lost prize gently into the farmer's big rough outstretched hand.

"I'm hungry. That's why I took it, it's only one egg."

The farmer's weather-beaten face softened a little as he looked at the boy and then up at Wode. "You're right, he's no leggit."

"Maybe, but he'll have a story. Shall we hear it?"

"Aye. I could do with a drink. Come into the kitchen, both of you. But keep an eye on him till I'm satisfied…

Oh, I'm Thrum by the way." He put out his hand.

"Wode," matching the farmer's strong grip. Thrum turned and walked off, examining the egg. Wode loosened his grip and the boy pulled his arm back, glaring up at his captor. Wode gestured for the boy to follow and closed the rear to block any escape. Not that he expected him to, but life's full of surprises, he thought, sighing, his recent solitude now only a memory, like the end notes of a beautiful song falling away into nothing.

---

The boy sat on a chair at the kitchen table, swinging one leg slowly backwards and forwards. His hands clasped the mug of warm milk and honey that Keela the farmer's wife had given him. He'd looked tired from his solo journey; he was wary and a little frightened, which brought Keela's maternal instincts to the fore. Her own boys were now old enough to help out around the farm and sometimes they were gone all day, leaving her to her chores and often to miss their boundless youthful energy.

Wode sat beside him, content with his own tea. Keela had provided him with a cup of hot water, into which he'd tapped some chopped, dried leaves from a small pouch.

He was listening intently to Thrum talk about the joys of running a farm.

"We've had some good years, Keela and I. The weather has been kind of late and our boys are old enough to make a difference to the workload. We always have more than enough. What more could a man ask for?" Glancing up fondly to catch Keela's eye.

"Nothing," agreed Wode. "Nothing at all."

Thrum sighed contentedly, quietly reflecting on his good fortune. A pause hung in the air like a feather suspended, patiently awaiting its time to fall to Earth. Keela spoke first.

"Are you Wode of Brennan?"

"Yes, Keela, I am."

She was looking at him with a mixture of awe, respect and sympathy.

"I'm sorry to hear about your wife and child." She paused. "Your reputation, as you can see, has travelled some. Are you on a solrom?"

He found sympathy difficult. "Yes."

"Ah."

There was a brief silence as Keela and Thrum looked at their visitor with renewed understanding and interest, their minds sifting this new information; they were used to gnoseers but Wode's reputation was in the early days of legend. The news of the double tragedy of his wife dying in childbirth and his son not even taking his first breath had reached even as far as Thrum and Keela at Athale.

After the death of his beloved Mara, Wode went through the motions of life – living off his smallholding, tending the sick and injured in his locale and working with the laws of nature and the universe for the greater good. Like all gnoseers, Wode had a deep understanding of human nature, a unique self-reliance in all realms – visible and invisible. But the chasm of grief was a place he'd not journeyed, and his karma had called him to solrom: to journey through his suffering and thread the weave of destiny to new purpose in his life.

Wode looked to deflect the attention. "And what about you, young man," turning to the boy. "Your name's not Jerreb, is it?" The younger's eyes widened in fear.

"You're more of a…" Wode broke off and went very still, as though listening to a whispering angel. "Geeter!" The boy was visibly stunned. "What about you?"

"How did you know my name?" he said breathlessly. Thrum had introduced him to Keela as Jerreb and they too were caught in the embrace of surprise.

Geeter regained his wits. "What about me?" he said petulantly.

Wode looked at him, ignoring his attitude. "How did you come to be out here, away from home – hungry and alone?"

"Have you run away?" asked Keela, concerned. The idea of a child running away from home appalled her.

Keela's softness melted Geeter's defiance and with the innocence of youth he unwrapped his past, as though carefully removing the leaves around the prickles of a hedgehog in its ball for winter sleep. Geeter's face grimaced with guilt and sadness as he related his story. He had left home soon after his mother had taken in another man. No one could replace his father and there were many arguments: his father had died from a fall in the mountains. He was a keen falconer and it was thought he'd fallen whilst trying to take a young eagle from its nest. His horse had made its riderless way home just before nightfall and neither Geeter nor his mother slept that night. A search party had gone out in the grey light before dawn and it was Geeter who'd led them to the nest site, knowing that was where his father had gone to capture a young life, and in doing so lost his own.

He was the first to see his hero father's lifeless body. His breathing faltered with the pain, his heart gripped by the fist of grief. They all watched in respectful silence as the tears rolled down his dusty cheeks in remembrance. Geeter looked up at Keela, a pleading in his eye to be relieved of his burden. Wode saw an image of a boy staggering down a deserted road carrying the weight of his father about his shoulders and leant towards him, putting a reassuring hand on his shoulder. "Go on, Geeter," he said gently.

Geeter told them about his father's burial and how all their friends and neighbours had rallied round and helped as he and his mother struggled on, united in their grief. But his mother was raised in a town and decided to move back with her parents for a while. It was there that her grief turned to anger and questions: why had he left her with a child to raise alone, why had Geeter not told her he was going out, she'd shouted, piercing the young boy's heart with her interrogation, their recent unity in grief beginning to part like cracks on a dried riverbed. His grandparents focused on comforting their daughter, and Geeter – who was still in shock – was struggling to come to terms with the loss of his beloved father and the move to a town away from all he had known and loved. Eventually his mother sold the farm he called home and bought a small house on the outskirts of Tulkney.

He had struggled with town life, missing the freedom of the hills – being able to roam in any direction without the claws of curious eyes. He loved being with the sheep on the hillsides, the cows in the pasturelands and exploring the crags and streams for fish and rabbits. And like his father, he loved birds. Wode's eyes narrowed imperceptibly as Geeter told of the hunting trips with his father and his falcons.

Geeter paused for a moment and Wode suddenly asked, "You dream of flying, don't you?"

"Yes," eyebrows raised in confused surprise.

"And you have the sensation of looking down at the ground as if in flight, like a bird?"

Geeter paused. "Yes."

Keela and Thrum looked at each other and Geeter shifted a little uncomfortably; his leg stopped swinging. He'd not even told his father about these incredibly vivid dreams that left him breathless with excitement and yet disturbed.

"Interesting…Go on, Geeter," said Wode gently.

He found Wode's tone reassuring and picked up his story. A dozen moon-cycles or so passed and Geeter wasn't making friends, and though his grandparents tried to help they were unable to reach him. His mother had cause to scold him more often and he felt isolated and angry. And then one lunchtime she brought home Sintle, a respected tailor in Tulkney, and Geeter could see he was keen on her. Each time Sintle visited he brought Geeter a little gift; he wasn't ungrateful, it was just that behind the action of giving, there was nothing else – an emptiness. Sintle seemed to expect that a gift was enough to gain friendship, respect and later on, obedience, and he hinted that Geeter would soon apprentice him in his shop. Over time, there was more talk of how he needed to choose a profession, make his way, contribute. Geeter's frustration grew; he had no idea what his future livelihood was to be but he was certain he wasn't going to be Sintle's apprentice. And then out of the blue his mother announced she and Sintle were to be married, and in no time he had moved in and was master of the house. In his mind, Wode could see the clash between Sintle and Geeter like bulls fighting over a herd: there was an invisible mantle conferred to a son on the death of his father – the right and responsibility of the archetypal provider for the family. Although too young to act out this instinctive rite, it was now part of him and it would have fuelled his conflict with Sintle.

Geeter's mother had tried to bring them together but all it did was to make her son resent her. He hated himself for it; he wanted everything to be all right but he couldn't help it. He was wounded; a hurt animal. Finally, he had reasoned, there was nothing else for it. It would be better for everyone if he left. Like all youngsters who run away, he'd not planned for the long term. He took his father's old pack, stuffed it with dried fruit, biscuits, bread and cheese, found his father's old ground blanket and staff and set off one promising dawn, protected by the ignorance and optimism of youth.

"I did all right for a week or two. It was dry and I had enough food, people were very kind but then the food ran out and I had to rely on what I could find and take." He paused, casting a glance at Thrum, who was sitting transfixed, full of sympathy and not without a little admiration for the boy.

"How long ago did you leave?" Thrum asked.

Geeter shrugged. "One moon-cycle, maybe one and a half. I'm not sure, I've been so tired and hungry it's difficult to remember."

"You've not got the longest legs. Tulkney's a long way…"

"I caught a ride with a trading caravan; a courier gave me a lift; some carts…people have been very kind."

"Are you going anywhere in particular, Geeter?" asked Keela.

"My uncle lives at Uik."

"You've a way still to go then."

There was the sound of approaching hooves and laughter. "The boys!" Keela got up suddenly. "Look at the shadows. It's getting late. You'll both have to stay here tonight. Thrum, get some hot water and show them where to wash. I'll make some supper and, Geeter, you can come and help me as soon as you've cleaned up."

"Come on, lad." Thrum picked up a large kettle that had been sitting by the fire and took him into the dairy. Wode followed.

"When was the last time you had a good wash?"

"I don't remember," Geeter grinned.

The two men exchanged a look of understanding, recalling happy childhood days getting filthy at play outside and being forced to clean up before sitting down to eat. The inconvenience of it!

As Wode and Geeter washed, they were joined by two strong-looking young men with a striking family resemblance.

"I'm Chet," said the younger.

"And I'm Jurdie."

"Wode, and this is Geeter."

"How do," they laughingly chorused and proceeded to get as much water on the floor as on themselves.

Geeter and Wode left them to it, rejoining Keela in the large stone kitchen. Geeter dutifully asked Keela what he could do to help and shortly found he had a knife in his hand and was being shown the vegetables.

Thrum came in. "Wode, will you come with me awhile?"

Wode nodded in agreement and followed him out of the door.

"I've got a horse that's lame," Thrum explained. "Would you mind having a look at it?"

"Not at all. Be a pleasure."

As they made their way down the hallway, Thrum suddenly stopped. He hesitated, looking at Wode with a mixture of uncertainty and compassion. Wode could see what was coming.

Finally Thrum cleared his throat. "I can understand, as a man, that to have lost your partner in life and your son must be devastating…I just wanted to say that."

"Thank you, Thrum, but I don't feel things like ordinary people," Wode replied, immediately realising he'd sounded a little cold and superior. "My gnoseer teacher once said, 'The gnoseer does not feel emotion like the ordinary man or woman because he knows the true purpose of life; his spirit must be free, unburdened, to pass through the eye of a needle when necessary. If he carries a shadow, its invisible weight will prevent his passage through all realms. You must be free to journey without regret for the past.'" He paused in recollection, a cascade of memories of his exacting training filling his mind. He continued as if he were still there, "I passed every test Worian put me through but it appears there is yet more for me to learn." He sighed, coming back to the present. "The grief comes in waves but I do not dwell on it, for to give it safe harbour is to darken my shadow, and you would be surprised at the weight of a mere absence of light."

Thrum stood a moment absorbing his words, humbled by the briefest of insights into this unusual man. "Thank you," he said, nodding, and turned to lead the way out of the house, grabbing a lantern to illuminate the darkness descending across the wide courtyard bounded by barn and byre.

He opened the door to a large stable and, in the illuminated gloom, Wode could see four horses eyeing them with calm curiosity.

"I would have thought they'd be out at this time of year: wolves?"

"Aye, but not a problem. No, they are inside at night to keep poor Sika company – herd animals, you understand."

"Yes of course. Is she your first mount?"

"Second. Keela rides her usually."

Whilst they were talking Wode was assessing the beautiful chestnut mare who stood still whilst the others came forward for carrots.

"She's a beauty. And in some considerable pain."

"Thought she might be. Can you see what happened?"

"Were you there at the time?"

"No."

Wode narrowed his eyes briefly and then simply stood there, trancelike, before sidling up to her, singing gently under his breath. He put his hand on her back and Thrum could see her visibly relax and watched fascinated as Wode went about his work. His soothing and barely audible song was making the other horses break off from their munching to turn and listen. His right hand moved along the mare's back and neck. He stopped at the top of her head and brought his left hand up to where his right had been, stepped closer, and ducked under her neck so that he had a hand either side of her head. She closed her eyes and began to sway in Wode's gentle hold, like a contented infant.

Thrum, riveted, looked on as Wode began to sway almost imperceptibly in time with Sika. It was as if the song was calling them out to its soothing rhythm: an ancient primal dance of man and beast. After what seemed like an age, Wode's hand slowly moved down to the injured fetlock and he sat down. He held the injured leg gently either side and closed his eyes. One of the other horses wandered over to sniff Wode's dark brown hair.

"Brun. Come on, leave him alone," Thrum said as he tugged the horse's head away.

"She's had a fright. Seen something that alarmed her and she twisted some sinews. Probably had all the weight on this leg at the time and turned in panic, with the hoof caught in a rut or hole. I don't think it is too serious. I will pack a poultice around the injury and she'll be right in a few days. If you could collect some of her urine somehow, it will help enhance the poultice."

"How much do you need?"

"Half a cupful should do it."

Wode returned his attention to the horse. He continued to sit there holding the injured fetlock and again began to sing quietly in a deep meditative voice. When the song ended, he sat there a few minutes longer as if far away and then got up slowly to pat Sika gently on the neck. He moved his head close to her muzzle and blew gently into her nostrils. She snorted back and tried to nibble his nose. Wode chuckled, stepping back.

"Thank you, Wode. I reckon you've earned your supper."

"Good thing. I'm so hungry, I could eat a horse." He turned to Sika. "Only joking, Sika. Only joking."

———

Candles and lanterns lit and the table set, there was a warm anticipation in the big stone kitchen as Keela brought the food to the table. Wode gave a thanksgiving for the food to be eaten and had to hold back from rushing it – such was his eagerness for the meal in front of him. Geeter had no such compunction and dived in, stuffing himself as quickly as he could. Thrum had produced a jug of cider made from last autumn's fall, which quickly brought a glow to the cheeks, and after the initial quietness of mouths full of food, loosened tongues turned to tales and stories. Chet and Jurdie told of their day – what they had seen of the outer reaches of the farm and the word from the shepherds and cowherds; they were the farmer's eyes and ears in the furthest reaches of his land.

Geeter simply sat there taking it all in, as did Wode, both enjoying the feeling of a full belly and the simple entertainment of family banter; Keela and Thrum delighting in their boys and the glow of hospitality – the knowledge of good giving.

———————

Wode and Geeter were to share a room upstairs at the back of the house. After supper they went out to retrieve Geeter's pack from where he'd left it hidden, a short distance from the farmhouse. It was a beautiful clear night and they both looked up at the stars as they walked, small steps beneath a vast twinkling black velvet shroud.

"Keela and Thrum are good people."

"Yes, they are. I feel bad about stealing an egg from them."

"Well, you didn't actually steal it, did you," said Wode with a wry smile.

"I know, I can't even get that right."

"Go easy on yourself, Geeter. And anyway you were attempting to fulfil a basic need for your body."

"What do you mean?"

"Your body was hungry and you were just doing your best to look after it. We are given a body to tread this earth, to experience the richness of life and fulfil our dreams. It helps to look after it."

"Yes, but I still feel I did wrong."

"I understand." Wode paused. "But tell me, why didn't you just knock at Keela's door and simply ask for an egg? That would have set up your karma better."

"What do you mean?"

"Karma? It's an ancient word that comes from lands far to the east, from the dawn of time. It is the invisible power behind the movement of life. It's destiny and...it's late, I'll have to explain it another time."

"But there may not be another time," Geeter said stubbornly.

"There will," he said in a voice to silence any dissent.

They found the pack. Wode picked up the blanket and staff and they retraced their steps.

Geeter looked up at his lofty companion. "It's strange. I hated you for catching me but I'm pleased somehow. Thank you."

Surprised, the gnoseer grunted in acknowledgement and patted the boy on the shoulder.

"We will talk tomorrow about your travels. But I am sure you can help out here for a few days, and there is always work for me."

"I'd like that."

"Good, I'll talk to Thrum and Keela."

Wode saw that Geeter was settled down to sleep before fixing the poultice to Sika's leg and returning to the fireside in the kitchen. The family were all enjoying another mug of cider and talking about what needed to be done over the next few days. Keela gestured for Wode to help himself from the jug.

"Is he asleep?"

"Nearly," said Wode, helping himself to a small cup. "He needs to decide what he is going to do now that he's been found. He has done well to make it this far alone. His father must have passed on good knowledge on their jaunts in the mountains."

"He needs to go back home to his mother, surely." Keela shivered at the thought of one of her sons going off at that age without any word.

"Well, he is young and he is intelligent. He set his course and he's the one that needs to steer his boat. It is his life to live – his karma." The others nodded in understanding as he spoke.

"His mother must be worried sick though," said Keela.

"She will surely be but she played her part."

Keela heard his tone but, emboldened by the cider, ventured to soften the gnoseer's view. "You are right of course but it does seem a bit harsh." Keela's imagination was being stirred by the instinct for her own brood.

"Harsh, perhaps…but just." Wode sighed. "Oh well, I can at least get the knowledge to her that he's all right."

"How?"

"Chet! You don't ask a gnoseer such things."

Wode smiled. "I don't mind, Thrum. I will answer Chet's question." The promise of such knowledge shared awoke their curiosity like a bored child eager for play; Jurdie stopped whittling a stick he'd been working; Keela even wondered if his need of a solrom had affected him: a gnoseer explaining how he performed his work in the inner realm was unheard of.

"I'll enter her dreams tomorrow night. She'll see an image of him happy and smiling and her worry will cease, although her concern won't – such is a mother's lot – and she will wake feeling easier but not knowing why."

"How will you enter her dreams?"

"Chet!" It was Keela's turn to be appalled, but she was also keen to hear Wode's answer.

"Through the deep formless inner realm that we are all connected to…and that's all I am going to tell you. But for it to work well, it would help if Geeter and I could spend a day or two in each other's company. It would enable me to build a strong connection to him. Could we stay a few days and work for our keep?"

"We'd be honoured to have you stay, Wode. And young Geeter."

"Thank you, that is kind of you," and with that he bade them goodnight, climbed the stairs and found his bed next to Geeter. He completed the nightly protective ritual that gnoseers do before sleep and reflected on the events of the day. He gave thanks for his good fortune and eventually allowed sleep to take him.

## Chapter 2

*You can learn anything with the right friend or teacher.*

They both waved as they made their way into the morning sun, the day's light of promise. Geeter walking backwards waving enthusiastically, feeling the pull of leaving the last happy few days behind, and Wode turning with one last gesture of thanks and farewell before setting his pace to a good rhythm to cover the ground. No sooner had he done so than he realised it might be too fast for the younger legs of his companion, and tempered the pace. A loner no more.

Their fresh legs soon made the top of the rise above the farmstead and they stopped to look back. Thrum was setting off for the pastures and Keela would no doubt be putting her house in order now her visitors had gone.

"Good people," said Wode. Turning back to scan the horizon, he took in the delightful undulations of the fertile land in all directions, the big river flowing deep and true to its end, the huge trees of ageless girth creating magnificent natural sculptures, and the highlands rising in the distance to the west where they were headed.

They had stayed a week. The farmers of Bracka were a hospitable lot and there was always work to be done to help out. There were also stories to be told, experiences to be shared and in the case of Geeter, a future to be considered. He'd been on the road about a moon-cycle, they had reckoned: time enough to sharpen wits and lose weight. This week had allowed him to lose his fear, build up some stamina and relax in the warm company of Thrum and Keela and the boys. Wode had pulled his weight but seemed to prefer his own company much of the time.

They walked in companionable silence, each with his thoughts of the past few days and what lay ahead. Wode had known soon after their first meeting that they were to travel together. Although just now he preferred his own company, having Geeter would be a good addition to his solrom, he thought – drawing him out of his internal roaming – and he had much he could teach him. Was he to have a young apprentice? He glanced sideways at Geeter. Geeter's mother was instrumental in her son's karma but it was up to Geeter himself and the Great Spirit to weave his purpose and destiny into a worthy life. Wode smiled to himself as Spirit had its ways of awakening seer potential in young men and women: sometimes after being struck by lightning where the brain was given such a surge, it wasn't uncommon for the enlightened to begin to see things others couldn't – moresight. Others were awakened by near-death events after travelling deep into the inner realms where only gnoseers dared to go voluntarily; and sometimes Life simply began to reveal the gifts in an individual over time, their karma creating circumstances for the individual to take notice.

Wode saw that Geeter had natural talent, that much was clear to him, but it was traditional in Brackan culture for it to be recognised by parents who would seek out an elder, sage or gnoseer for advice and possible apprenticeship. There were many noble ways to serve Bracka's people and often the young man or woman would be guided by their Spirit within – sensing the influence of their disposition – and it was incumbent upon the elder being consulted to help them recognise, develop and use their gifts for the benefit of all. That was the way it was. Brackans knew everyone had talents and not all were obvious. Growing these gifts in a young person made them stronger and happier, and this growth benefited everyone; some talents remained dormant like a seed, waiting for the right conditions to start it into life. Wode smiled to himself: he would enjoy helping Geeter realise his gifts.

---

They'd been going for an hour with few words between them, Wode mainly passing comment on the birds, insects and animals they saw. He was not only appreciating the natural beauty around him, as gnoseers tended to do, but also assessing Geeter's reactions and interest. Geeter was certainly moved as all young people were by nature, but he was especially moved by the birds, tilting his head to best catch the message in their songs and closely following the nuance of their flight.

"Geeter, what is it about birds that holds your interest?"

Geeter looked at the gnoseer guardedly. He wasn't entirely relaxed in Wode's presence but he found that he felt safe enough to be truthful. "When I was little I thought I was a bird."

"Tell me."

"Well…" Geeter hesitated.

"Go on, I am interested," encouraged Wode.

"Well, it sounds a bit silly."

Geeter paused, looked into the distance and caught sight of a black kite slowly circling as it scanned the ground for prey. "I…" He stopped. "It's just that, when I was little, I used to think I was a bird…because it was as if I could look down from up high, as you said the other night."

"And you weren't just looking down from a rock or tree."

"No, I was moving, sort of gliding, and I could almost feel the wind over my wings…um, arms."

"Interesting." Wode was silent for a while. Geeter continued to watch the kite, as if in a trance, noticing the small movements of tail and wing, effortless adjustments to the currents of air, the vagaries of wind.

"And now, do you still see the ground from the same height?"

"Yes, but only when my eyes are closed and I'm sort of relaxed, and in my dreams."

"Good."

"Why?" Wode saw Geeter's eyes gleaming with interest. There was hesitancy too. Geeter had confided in his mother once, only to be told he was making it up and not to bother her with such flights of fancy. She'd giggled at her own wit as she left Geeter feeling slightly hurt and foolish.

"Well, you have something of the spirit of bird in you. You have a natural disposition towards our feathered cousins – an affinity. You feel a bit like a bird and you see a bit like a bird. Does that make sense to you?"

"I'm not sure."

"Don't worry, you'll see for yourself. We will call in the birds." Wode removed his pack and, after a brief rummage, pulled out some dried trout and bread. He broke two bits off each and packed the rest away. "Hold a piece in each hand – fish in one, bread in the other. I'll do the same."

"What for?"

"Wait and see." Wode paused. "Now close your eyes, take a few deep breaths…feel your feet…connect to the earth…and be still, go beyond your mind…to the birds. Hang on to the idea of calling them in for the food that you have for them. You've got flesh for any raptors, and bread for the others. You can hear them in the sky, trees and bushes; connect what you hear – inside you – and send your presence back out to the source of the sounds. And let's see what happens."

There was silence as Geeter concentrated hard, frowning. Nothing happened.

"Geeter, you are trying too hard."

"But I don't know what to do," he shot back.

"So assess the response you got to how you were, change yourself, your approach. Do something different and the outcome will change." Wode remembered Geeter talking of his stepfather Sintle and realised that his own tone might have sounded too similar, expecting obedience. He softened his voice. "Take a deep breath, relax and smile as you do this. Just take the idea of what I told you, don't think about it. Go to that place within where you go to see like a bird. You are going into the vast space within you, beyond your understanding."

Wode watched Geeter fill his lungs and position an uncertain smile on his young face. Wode relaxed his eyes and studied the boy's aura. Silently he moved behind him and made some adjustments. Geeter sighed, and his smile broadened.

"That's it, be patient. Wait. Send out your welcome and let them come…Good. I'll do the same."

Wode moved away and stood beside him. Luckily, thought Wode, there were no folk passing on the drover's road, as he and Geeter would have made a strange pair standing side by side, smiling away with arms akimbo.

Wode opened his eyes a moment to check on his young companion and closed them again to reach out to the birds also. As he tuned in, he opened his eyes but held the calm, quiet inner state of communication. He saw the black kite was now circling above them and he could hear an increase in the small birds' twitter in a nearby tree. He could tell they wanted to come but were cautious because of the kite.

Suddenly, "Oh!" The kite swooshed past, close to Geeter's head. He opened his eyes in surprise, and stood transfixed in delight. The bird circled again very close and then turned towards them once more, slowing right down with a backwards tilt to its gliding wings as it nimbly removed the bit of dried trout from Geeter's hand.

"Ohhh! Wode…incredible!"

The kite had flown off a way to transfer the fish from talon to beak, and with one swallow it was circling back with interest in Wode's morsel. Again, but with more trust this time, it swooped close by and then, reassured, returned for its prize.

Climbing away to circle higher, clutching the second trout morsel, it again transferred from talon to mouth and gave out a distinctive gree-er si-si-si-si-si.

"You are welcome," Wode replied. "Now Geeter, let the kite go and then bring your arms up and hold steady, relax, take a deep breath and keep your attention on inviting the bread eaters in. With the black kite gone, the others will come. Crumble the bread into crumbs first though."

Geeter did as he was told and stood there, brow furrowed. Nothing happened.

"Remember, stop trying: let go of any effort. Your trying is pushing your energy. The 'push' will put them off. It is not gentle enough. Let go of all wanting for it to happen…Feel your feet make connection to the earth… Good, that's it. And simply wait."

Soon enough, one, then two beautiful little yellow-green-striped finches circled Geeter. One landed on his head and another on his shoulder. Then a few more landed on his outstretched hands. He chuckled in delight. Wode had one or two quietly pecking from his hand but not as many as Geeter.

"Goodness! Wode. This is…How is it happening?"

"You have a gift with birds, my young friend. They know you sense a oneness with them and they feel completely safe in the spirit of your presence that you are emanating."

"Really?"

"Clearly, and now you know you will never be alone." Wode frowned, not sure why he'd said that.

"I can't wait to show my mother."

Wode glanced at him. "Mmm."

"What is 'emanating'?"

Wode reflected a moment, considering his audience. "You've thrown pebbles into a still pond, causing ripples?" Geeter nodded. "The ripples are emanating out from the splash. When the sky is thundering, you can feel

the vibrations of sound emanating out from the boom.
Well, so it is at a more subtle level with everything in
creation. Everything has its own vibration, or resonance.
When you say a word or think any thought, it has a spirit
that emanates out from you all around, into the universe.
You know when someone is angry because you feel and
sense it as well as seeing anger on their face, and you
will no doubt want to get away from them. In some of
the taverns in the big towns you can hear men swearing
and going on. The spirit of the words they use is pretty
ugly, and you will want to remove yourself from the area
because you have felt the low spirit and emanation of
their words. And the opposite is true; you will feel drawn
to be with happy, contented folk and want to spend more
time in their good company because they are emanating
a natural ease and joy – like Thrum and Keela. And that
is what you were doing with the birds – emanating the
spirit of your presence, which they are attracted to. We
all have gifts and talents, if we can only discover and use
them – in this way we are all equal. And you have a gift
with birds."

"I like that."

"And so you should," chuckled Wode.

"Can I do it with animals?"

"With time and practice, Geeter, perhaps, if you train to be a gnoseer. I wanted you to experience this bit of magic that you have to help you over the journey ahead. Now we must get going, we have some ground to cover."

Wode swallowed some water from his flask. Geeter grabbed his pack and staff and came to stand beside him. The gnoseer had allowed him into his inner circle and the privilege was not lost on him. He felt taller, even older somehow, and an unfamiliar sense of purpose was stirring in him, like an early spring bud foretelling a leafy promise. He looked at the road ahead and then up at Wode, who nodded, and they stepped out in unison.

---

It was while they were sitting around the kitchen table with Thrum and Keela on the second night that Wode had gently brought up Geeter's immediate future for consideration. It was obvious the boy was feeling some guilt about how his mother might be feeling, as at times he was surly and defensive. It was a desperate heart that had made him leave but a defiant spirit had kept him going, and his destiny was calling him onwards through time.

"What do you want to do, Geeter?"

There was a pause. "I want to stay here. I'll work hard," he implored.

Keela and Thrum looked at each other. It was Keela who spoke with compassion. "No, Geeter. You need to go back to your mother."

"But *he's* there!" he shouted.

"Yes, but maybe Wode could do something about him." She glanced at Wode who shook his head saying, "I'm not interfering."

"Then I shall continue on my way to Uik," Geeter said imperiously, ringing the bell of confidence with a discordant clang.

"Your mother will be concerned about you and no doubt wracked with guilt. She deserves an explanation. Even for just suffering the pain of your entry into the world," Keela added.

Geeter looked at Wode who said nothing, and then at Thrum who was nodding in agreement.

"It's my life. I've done really well by myself."

"Indeed you have, but did you consider how the next year, two years or more, would turn out?" said Wode with a sternness forged in his recent travails, and looking deeply into Geeter's eyes.

"Well…I just thought…No, I suppose not."

Geeter wriggled in his seat, not used to such power from a look.

Wode softened his voice. "Would it not be the right thing to do to speak to your mother and talk to her about your future?"

"Yes, I suppose so," Geeter's defiance conceding to compassion and reason.

"Good. Well if it is all right with our kind hosts, we might be able to stay a further few days. Fatten you up and help around the farm and then you and I will go to Tulkney to talk to your mother."

Geeter grinned and everyone looked from one to the other, Keela and Thrum both pleased and assessing each other's thoughts – considering the longer stay, the opportunity for Geeter to spend time with a highly regarded gnoseer, and the benefits to them too.

"You stay as long as you like," Keela chuckled.

---

After a further two hours of walking Wode started looking for a place to rest and eat. He picked a large tree with plenty of shade from the heat of the late spring sun, beside a stream with a series of pools.

"Can you make us a fire, Geeter? I'm going to see if there's a fresh trout in the stream. And give me your flask, I'll fill it up."

As Geeter was squatting down trying for a spark on the dry-leaf bundle he'd scraped together, he looked up to see Wode tossing a wriggling trout onto the bank. "That was quick," he muttered and redoubled his efforts with the fire.

Finally Geeter had a flame moving through the dry leaves and he gently added some twigs and sticks. Blowing from several angles to get an even burn, he blinked away the smoke which seemed to follow him from one side to the next, and sat back to admire his handiwork. He was sitting staring into the dancing flames when Wode joined him with two sizeable fish that he'd already gutted, leaving the innards on the bank for the birds. "Good fire, Geeter," he said as he set about fashioning a simple spit between two forked sticks in the ground.

"You know how to gut a fish, don't you?"

Geeter nodded. "Yes, my father taught me, and how to pluck and draw a bird too."

"Good. Put a couple of potatoes into the ash and we will have those after the fish."

They ate hungrily and afterwards Wode settled down for a brief nap, but not before seemingly stroking the air in an arc from above his head to the ground and then doing something similar towards Geeter. Geeter unrolled his blanket too and, though slightly puzzled by Wode's ritual, settled down beside him without comment. It wasn't long before both were fast asleep; the world is a better place after lunch.

---

"What's a gnoseer, Keela? I mean, I've heard of them in stories but I've never met one before."

They were in the kitchen preparing the evening meal together. Geeter had helped his mother in the past and so was quite familiar with doing what a lot of men and boys would call women's work.

"Well, Geeter, that is a good question. They have skills and ways that stretch back into the mists of time. Some say even to the great Beginning." Keela focused on washing a potato as she considered how best to answer him.

"Of course you are better off asking Wode but I can see why you are starting with me." She smiled. "They are men and women who see, hear or just know things that most of us do not. They work with the powers of the universe to give of themselves to heal and help us all. Some travel and some just serve the people in their locale. They are close to nature and some say they can take the form of an animal, travel through time and change the past to change the present or future."

"Goodness!"

"Yes, I know. Best not to annoy them!"

"Tell me more, Keela."

"Well, they are very wise and are usually the ones called to the Wisdom Tree."

"What's the Wisdom Tree? I mean, I've heard of that too

– my father mentioned it, I think – but I'm not sure. It isn't talked of in Tulkney."

"No, town folk are losing touch with the old ways, and it will be their undoing," Keela sighed.

"The Wisdom Tree is the biggest mystery on Bracka. It grows in the middle of the island, in the central fertile lowlands of the Tulrain, not far from Kuik. It's the only tree of its type found anywhere and they say it's half as old as time. It's huge and mysterious."

Geeter was agog. "Half as old as time?"

"Indeed. And underneath the Wisdom Tree sits the Keeper – a sage or gnoseer. They are sometimes there for a week, a fortnight or even just a day. Folk go to the Wisdom Tree for advice, to seek knowledge, and the amazing thing is, it doesn't matter when they go, the right sage or gnoseer will be there to give them the perfect answer to their question! A particular gnoseer will just get an intuition, a calling within that they need to leave whatever they are doing and travel to the Tree of Knowledge – its other name. And there they sit and wait, answering questions from anyone who has travelled to ask. Lore has it that they only leave when the next one turns up. But the truth is, no one knows because you don't go to the Tree without a question, and as the right sage is already there, no one has ever turned up to find themselves alone there. Once your question is answered you go on your way." She paused, remembering her own visit many years ago to the Tree. "It has massive boughs extending out forty feet, tapering into lovely long, soft needles. It's maybe two hundred feet high and in perfect condition. No rot, no lightning or wind damage. Perfect!"

Geeter was all ears, his imagination conjuring a magical picture of the great Tree.

"It's protected, of course: it is said that whosoever should damage the Tree, take a branch, or carve their name on the trunk, will be cursed with a thousand ills that not even the most powerful gnoseer could heal. You can pick its flowers though, if you are tall enough; in summer it has the most heavenly scent and from the flowers you can make the most delicious tea – although most daren't. But I bet Wode has some in his tea pouch."

"So what sort of questions do people ask?"

"Anything really. But something significant. You aren't going to travel for days just to ask how to grow cabbages!"

Geeter laughed. Then he was suddenly silent. Keela knew what was coming next.

"I could go there and ask about my future, couldn't I?"

"Yes, you could."

———————

The sound of hooves and the creaking of a cart had Wode awake and on his feet in seconds. Leaving his bedroll, he ran to the side of the road, arriving in time for the horses to see him without being alarmed. He put up his hands and the driver, a big man rising out of his seat like a town square statue, pulled on the reins to bring the horses to a stop.

"Greetings, sir."

"Greetings to you too. Do you want a ride?"

"Thank you, and I have a young lad with me."

"There's room enough."

"I'll just get our packs."

Wode called out to Geeter who was by now awake.

"Come on, we've got a ride." The fire had died down but Wode doused it with water from the stream to make it safe while Geeter rolled up their blankets.

"Where are you headed?" asked the man, all barrel chest and heavy brow.

"Tulkney."

"I'm going into Kellin to sell my skins. You'll have to get in the back, young'un, there's only space for one more up here."

Geeter walked round to the back of the cart and got a whiff of the freshly tanned rawhides. He swallowed hard and clambered up to sit carefully on a wagon board not covered by the simple leather. He held his nose to start with but the breeze helped and he soon became used to the smell.

Seeing him settled, Wode climbed up front and thanked the driver, who nodded and stirred his horses.

## Chapter 3

*Anything is possible if the thing you
call "I" is out of the way.*

They travelled for two days as a threesome, and Carg
the tanner enjoyed the company – especially Geeter's. At
times the trips to Kellin were lonely so he often picked
up travellers for entertainment and to gather news. Some
were great fun and others not so easy but he'd never
been threatened or had the horses stolen. He'd picked
up the odd gnoseer before; they were a different lot
and often seemed more introverted than your average
man or woman. He'd never understood them but then,
he reasoned, normal folk probably weren't supposed to
understand gnoseers or their ways. He liked to pass the
time but he'd found Wode somewhat impenetrable.

"I do like to get away," Carg said on the morning of the second day.

There was a pause. "Oh yes?" Wode was less given to small talk.

"Yes, I can give my ears a break."

Another pause. "Why's that?"

"Well, it's the wife – she nags a bit."

"Really?"

"Yes, and she can go on a bit too."

"Mmm."

"Yes, the ears can get a right ringing."

There was a brief silence during which Wode weighed up the consequences of responding – knowing he would probably offend but at least he would get some peace for a while.

"Forgive me, Carg, but what if your wife has a point?"

"What? What do you mean?"

"Well, you are suggesting to me that you like a quiet life and yet you are obviously giving your wife cause to complain. The intelligent thing to do would be to stop doing what she complains about, or do what you are not doing that she complains about, and your ears will have a holiday."

"I don't follow you."

"You are making your wife nag."

"Don't be daft. She does it without any help from me!" Carg was used to men picking up the cue and joining in with a general round of complaints about women, rising prices, inclement weather, scraping a living and general worldly woes. He wasn't used to his cues being ignored, let alone tossed back like a hot potato into his lap.

"Would you like her not to nag?" Wode said, without a hint of exaggerated patience.

"Course I would," Carg said firmly.

"Would it improve your life if she didn't do it ever?"

"Yeees."

Carg was suspicious now, his simple intellect groping the darkness of ignorance for the hidden trap, like a bull being led by its nose into a camouflaged cattle pen.

"Well you have it in your power to stop the nagging."

Carg shot a sideways look at Wode. "How's that then?"

"Do as she asks," said Wode, closing the pen's gate behind him.

"What, go under her thumb?" Carg spluttered.

"Look, you run your trade as a tanner and you have help to do it."

"Yes, a couple of lads."

"Do you want to run your home as well?"

"NO! That's women's work."

"So she is in charge of running the home, the same way as you are in charge of the tanning. If your apprentice lads did not do something you asked them to, you'd have good reason to nag them, wouldn't you?"

Carg opened his mouth to respond but shut it again soundlessly. He was a good sort and got the point. Wode could sense the tanner's internal huffing and puffing as he pondered his words in silence, and smiled, gratefully returning his attention to examining the passing countryside.

Now and then Wode would ask Carg to halt the horses – "medicinal plants", he'd say by way of explanation, jumping down to examine a plant closely. More often than not, he would start talking to the plant and then pause.

Intrigued, finally Geeter jumped down too.

"What are you talking to the plant for?"

"I'm asking its permission."

"Permission for what?"

"To take off some leaves that it has been growing."

"Oh," said Geeter in a "fair enough" sort of way.

He watched Wode pause as if to wait for an answer and then carefully remove some leaves and place them into a rolled-up cloth that came from the depths of his pack bag.

"It's important to thank the plant too," Wode said to Geeter and turned to do just that.

Later, in the middle of the day when they had stopped to rest the horses, Geeter and Wode went off to climb a hill to look out a stream in which to catch some trout.

"Wode?"

"Yes."

"My mother used to nag. I didn't catch all of what you were saying to Carg…"

"Why do you think your mother was nagging?"

"Oh, I don't know. It was normally because I didn't do things as quickly as she'd have liked."

"Do her eyebrows slant upwards from the centre?"

"Don't know. Why?" said Geeter, a little puzzled.

"People with eyebrows that slant upwards from the nose like to get things done first and then rest afterwards. Whereas those of us with flat eyebrows are a bit more relaxed and will do things in our own time."

"How do you know?"

"Basic face reading. I might teach you it someday. But back to your mother." He took a deep breath. "There will be two things going on: firstly your mother will have had some worries, and secondly, people will emanate their emotions into the world and usually onto those around them – family." He pointed to Geeter. "And so you are going to get the butt of her internal frustration, anxiety or anger. It is just the way it is with emotional people."

They had reached the hill's summit and Wode scanned around for the telltale sign of a snake of trees growing beside a meandering watercourse.

"And secondly, do you remember when I spoke of karma?"

"Yes," Geeter nodded.

"This might not be easy to grasp, but just hear me out." Wode paused, looking into the distance. "Because you have chosen your current life and existence, it means you are responsible for everything that happens in it. You have heard the expression 'As you sow, so shall you reap'?" Geeter nodded. "Well in the case of your mother nagging you, you were not being responsible. She had asked you to do something and you had not done it; you had gone off to please yourself – playing with friends, for example. Now I know it is difficult with parents sometimes but if you are asked to do something by someone in authority or guardianship over you, assuming it is a reasonable request, then you should do it if you are to be honest. And if you don't, then you are not being honest with her and you must take the consequences. So the question is, why not? What is it in you that is distracting you from what you have been asked to do? So I was gently prodding Carg because it is what he is doing, or not doing, that is causing his wife to nag. Therefore he is doing it – it is of his own making!"

"I can see why Carg went quiet," Geeter said. Wode chuckled.

Geeter continued, "And what do you mean, 'chosen my current life'?"

"Aaaah, Life's mystery." Wode was pleased with Geeter's intelligent questions.

"Well, your life is like a river making its unique journey to the sea. You are forging a way with no course and no banks – they come behind you as your past, your mark. When you were very young, you were a clear, carefree stream just tumbling down the mountain with your parents to guide you. And as you go through your life, your soul – the being that you are deep inside you –

guides your life-flow to find the best course to the sea, through the events that shape your life – your karma – to your ultimate destiny. As you flow you gather your own life experience as more water, and the wisdom and guidance of others flow into you like tributaries. Your impact on the earth will deepen; challenges will arise like big rocks and you will need to find the best way past – sometimes flowing in a different direction but always flowing, like time. Now the rocks and challenges in life are placed there by you…I'll explain." Wode saw Geeter frown.

"When your body dies, Life carries your soul as it flows into the vast sea – the ocean of eternal life. Here in this fathomless place of wonder and love, you go and find your depth – to rest and assimilate. It is not a place of one depth; there are vast depths as deep as the highest mountains are high, and beyond. Here, without your body, you are simply spirit – a Soul Being – and you begin to examine the course your river of life weaved to the sea. Did you flow as well around challenges as you could have? Could you have learnt more, helped others on their course more and so on. This time of assimilating and absorbing goes on until you have gathered all that you could have received from the life just lived. This, is true alchemy."

Geeter was spellbound by the gnoseer's words; the secrets of the universe flowing out of Wode to envelop his mind in a warm embrace of its timeless mystery.

"The purpose of karma is to give us experiences in our life. Within each experience there is a golden essence for us to gather, and as we integrate this essence into our soul between lives, we transform it into light." Wode pointed to Geeter's chest. "Because inside you, young Geeter, is a gathering star. And once you have transformed enough essence into light, over many lifetimes, that is what you become. But until then, when you have completed the transformation of your recent life's essence into light, there comes a point of completion and you begin to yearn to exist in a body again, to have more of the great mystery revealed through another life – another river's journey. At this stage you decide what to learn in the next life's experience, remembering that it is the challenges and hardships that shape us the most; the Great Spirit our Source reveals the potential in two or three possible lives we could live that it has prepared for us – rivers flowing in different parts of the world, with different guides as tributaries and new, potentially rocky challenges – as karma – for us to face. When we have decided which life will best serve our learning and growth, we rise to the surface of the Great Sea and on into the air to become cloud. The Great Wind carries us to where we are destined to be and, when the time is right, we fall as rain and begin our flow all over again."

Geeter thought awhile. "So we are a soul in a 'river' body which is flowing down to the sea?"

"It is a way of seeing it, yes."

"It is really us wearing a body for our journey, like we put on fine clothes for festivals."

Wode nodded, impressed. "Yes, exactly, or like the travelling players who don costumes to play a part on the stage. And there's another aspect to karma you should know about. In the life you choose, certain lessons are destined to come your way – the rocks in your river's path – and if you avoid those lessons, those experiences destined for your gathering essence, when they first come, they will return to you later in a different guise and you will have to face them again. It is more fortuitous to deal with them rightly when they first come, so your life gets easier and less challenging. Or you can just back everything up to face later in life, but that is just asking for trouble.

"Now being responsible – this is still karma – is also about what you emanate into the inner realm: it is this inner space – where you think and dream – which connects us all. And it is because we have this inner space that our thoughts and ideas and inspirations stand out." Geeter looked puzzled.

"See that rock there." Wode pointed to a large boulder to his left. Geeter nodded. "The reason you can see it as rock is because of the space around it."

Geeter pondered a moment. "So I know I'm thinking when I see a thought as different to the inner space around it."

Wode looked sharply at Geeter. "You catch on fast. That is exactly right, Geeter. Well done."

Geeter looked pleased and faintly embarrassed to receive praise.

"So if you are thinking negative thoughts and having negative feelings, these emanate all around and into that inner space – and the inner realm has one universal law: it gives back what you put in. This is why negative people always seem to be negative and positive people, positive – what they put in they get back. It is best to put goodness into the great karmic wave, for us and for all. But we can all become stuck in mental-habit patterns within, so our living life – without – is to teach us to get out of them."

Geeter absorbed this a moment. "So is this why you are on a solrom — to change your karma somehow?"

"Yes, Geeter." Wode paused. "A solrom is a journey to heal within, by going without."

Geeter thought some more. "Are you trying to teach me?"

Wode looked at Geeter, aware that his answer had reach into the future. "You ask intelligent questions. One can only pour wisdom into a receptive ear."

"But you have to want to give of your knowledge."

"Yes. I had a son, you see, but..." Wode lapsed into silence, looking off into the distance, a brief sadness passing through him. He looked down at Geeter to see him smiling up at him, beaming from ear to ear. Wode raised his eyebrows questioningly.

"I'm smiling you," Geeter explained. "Putting smiling into my inner realm to emanate."

Wode was touched by his young companion's spirit. "Thank you, Geeter. Well, I don't see a stream so we had better get back to Carg and the horses, or he will leave without us."

They started off down the hill in companionable silence. Geeter was absorbed in himself; there was something stirring deep within him and he was aware of a sense of space expanding in his chest. He looked up at Wode. "Why are you teaching me?"

Wode studied him briefly. "Because you are here, because it is your karma and because you need to understand the mystery of Life."

---

Without fish for lunch Wode had shared out the remaining food Keela had packed them and they'd all had a good rest, giving the horses plenty of time to pull at the long spring grass. Refreshed, they'd set off again to cover as much ground as possible in the afternoon, and they were now making good speed, travelling through wide-open forest glades that broke up large areas of dense woodland – of birch and pine, with occasional pockets of oak. Carg was just muttering about finding a place to stop for the night when Wode suddenly stiffened beside him, senses alert. "There's something coming this way…"

There was a low pounding hum to their right – hooves beating the earth, legs crashing through undergrowth, travelling fast. The horses were immediately tense, sensing panic, and as they came to a small bend bordered with thick undergrowth a large herd of deer burst through onto the road, running for their lives. The horses reared up with hooves slashing the air in front of them as they tried to turn away from the danger, bringing the cart to an immediate crashing halt.

Wode was moving faster than time, vaulting off the cart as Carg was fighting for control of the reins. The instant his feet touched the ground Wode was turning instinctively to check on Geeter, who was in mid-air, being catapulted off the back of the cart – somersaulting helplessly to land in a crumpled heap.

"Wolves!" Carg shouted as the horses reared again in sheer fright, throwing him forward onto the nearest horse's rump. Wode whipped round to face the danger. He counted eight, the lead wolf keeping the chase fast, tiring their prey, his teeth flashing yellow-white in the late-afternoon sun as he kept up the deadly pursuit. Wode watched in relief as the pack, entirely engrossed in pursuing the panicked herd, seemed to ignore them completely. Only then was he aware of his heart pounding as he ran to grab the horses and settle them enough for the winded Carg to slide down off the horse's back. Wode was holding on tight to the flailing reins. The horses, with ears frantically scanning for sounds of danger and eyes wide, searching for a predator's charge, were looking to bolt.

"Carg. Come and take over here, will you?"

Wode held on and the horses began to calm with his soft words of reassurance. The tanner came up and took the reins; he was panting heavily.

"I need to check on Geeter. Can you hold them?"

Carg nodded, unable to speak, and Wode hurried past the cart to where Geeter was lying very still, eyes staring skywards, fixed on nothing. Wode felt a pang of concern as he knelt down. "Can you hear me?"

Geeter's eyes swivelled slowly towards him. "Yes."

"Where does it hurt?"

Geeter paused, assessing through his shock. "All over."

"Anywhere in particular?" Wode was judging the situation; he'd seen Geeter land heavily on his left side.

"My shoulder."

"Don't worry lad, we'll get you right. I'm just going to see if there is anywhere else you are hurt." Wode frowned in concentration as he began scanning Geeter's energy, his hand hovering a couple of inches above his body. He was feeling for energy shocks – areas of chaotic swirling like invisible mirages. Here and there he would touch Geeter when he sensed something, and look at his face for any reaction.

"You bounce well, Geeter. It seems the force of the impact was all taken by your arm and shoulder. I had better have a look at it." He looked around. "I am going to help you up and move you off the road to somewhere a bit more comfortable. Get up onto all fours first, and then we'll go from there."

Keeping his left side immobile and with Wode's help, Geeter was slowly able to find a kneeling position. Wode stood up and, gently supporting him under his right shoulder, helped him to stand.

"Well done," said Wode encouragingly. Geeter, ashen-faced, smiled weakly and allowed Wode to guide him gently off the road. "Can you stand unaided?" Geeter swayed a little as Wode let go with hands hovering to help him, but he nodded. Satisfied, Wode left him briefly to retrieve his blanket and lay it on a soft bed of needles under a majestic old pine.

"Let's get you comfortable," said Wode, helping Geeter down to winces and gasps of pain. Once Geeter was settled, Wode retrieved his pack and began rummaging around inside, pulling out his medicine bundle. He tapped some mixture into his hand and reached for his water flask.

"Open wide." Geeter complied like a young bird receiving a worm from its parent, and Wode tipped the herbal powder into the boy's open mouth. Geeter grimaced at the taste.

"Here, you will need some water," he said, handing him the flask. Geeter screwed up his face and swallowed hard. "Good lad. Now lie back."

"What happened?"

"Wolves chasing deer. A big herd."

Wode reached for his knife and began to cut away Geeter's shirt. Wode looked up. "No blood, Geeter. That's the good news." But the arm was no longer straight above the elbow.

Carg came up. "How is he?"

"Broken arm, just below the shoulder."

Carg looked down at the injury and wished he hadn't. He felt himself going pale and with a sharp intake of breath, winced in imagined pain. "What you going to do?"

"Put it back together again."

"But we can't stay here. We're in the wolves' territory."

"He is in no fit state to sit on a moving wagon, and the wolves will not be back this way. They'll be feasting on fresh deer meat a mile or two away by now."

"And what if the deer got away from them, eh? They'd still be hungry, wouldn't they!"

Wode grinned up at Carg. "I'd better get to it then. Don't worry," he said reassuringly. "Trust me, we will be fine, but you had better keep a look-out." Carg harrumphed and went off to check his cart over and lead the horses off the road to find grass.

Wode reached into his pack and carefully removed a leather pouch. He held it reverently in both hands before placing it on his lap and drawing from within the most beautiful, clear, flawless crystal Geeter had ever seen. Wode examined it carefully. He never failed to be moved by its perfectly straight faceted sides – eight of them graduating down to the finest points at each end. Turning it slowly in the sunlight sent flashing beams of rainbow colours hither and thither, like merrily dancing faeries on the trees and undergrowth around them. The size of a large knife handle, it fitted perfectly into Wode's hand, and pulling himself away from its mesmerising beauty, he placed it gently into Geeter's left hand and slowly squeezed his fingers around it, holding it in place. Wode then put a blanket over Geeter's chest and legs and settled himself into a comfortable position.

"All right, Geeter?"

Geeter gave him a brave smile through the pain, and Wode nodded, then brought his hands to hover either side of the broken limb. The boy watched at first with a mixture of curiosity and suspicion, but he trusted the gnoseer completely and after a few seconds, closed his eyes.

"That's it, you relax. Take some deep breaths. I am just connecting with your energy body and then I am going to gently support and hold your arm." Geeter felt a sense of warmth flooding the injured shoulder and then a strange tingling before he felt himself drifting away into a deep recuperative sleep.

Wode remained beside him holding the arm, and they stayed like that for as long as it took for the shadows to lengthen and disappear. Then, just as the sun dipped behind the hill, there was movement beneath Wode's hands, a twisting.

Geeter's eyes suddenly opened wide in surprise as he felt the bone move behind his bicep. There was a huge surge of energy like a vast unstoppable ocean wave rolling down his arm, through his wrist and hand, and into the crystal; and then nothing but the feeling of silence. The pain had vanished, and there was complete stillness.

With a satisfied smile on his face, Wode squeezed Geeter's arm gently and then let go.

Geeter gasped in astonishment. "What was that?"

"The bone realigning itself."

Geeter was suddenly aware of his hand. "The crystal's burning."

"It's holding the force of the impact." Wode removed it from Geeter's grip and swiftly returned it to its pouch.

Geeter looked quizzical. "How did you do it?"

"It's a bit of an explanation."

"You have to tell me."

Wode looked over towards Carg, who was napping under a tree. He thought for a second and then smiled at Geeter with a nod. "Well, as a gnoseer I can change someone's karma and facilitate their healing without disrupting the natural order of things. That is my privilege, but only if it is going with the flow of their life."

"How?"

"I went deep into the inner realm where it is timeless. And then I synchronised your energy with mine – sort of travelled back in time to the point before your bone was broken. Thus the force of the trauma had to come out, and it did so - as heat."

Geeter lit up. "I want to be able to do that."

Wode knew that Spirit had arranged this healing demonstration for a purpose. "And perhaps you will."

"Will you teach me?"

"Maybe, but it depends on your mother. Now that is enough talk. Let's get you ready for the road, young fellow."

Wode reached into his healing bundle for an ointment for Geeter's arm. He applied it gently, and then bound some cloth around it, fashioning a sling to keep it secure. Satisfied, he picked up the leather pouch and got up on stiff legs. He walked away a short distance, then faced the setting sun and pulled a small bottle from an inner pocket. He uncorked it, took a swig and, holding the liquid in his mouth, removed the crystal from its pouch.

From where he sat, Geeter watched the cleansing ritual in silence, with interested eyes taking in every movement. Wode faced the south and held the crystal a few inches from his mouth and spat out a clear liquid over the crystal and muttered a few words. He turned west, north and east, repeating the process. After each direction, he 'listened' to the crystal's emanation through his hand, sensing how clear the crystal was becoming after absorbing the energy of Geeter's injury. After facing the east, he appeared satisfied and returned the crystal to its home.

Wode stood for a moment more with eyes closed and then wandered over to join Carg, who was now awake and sitting up under the tree.

"He can manage the ride now and we should press on a bit further to the night's camp."

"Really? I hardly think…" Carg started, but then broke off in disbelief as he saw Geeter getting up and walking towards the cart, flexing his left arm experimentally out of the sling. "Well," he spluttered, "right then." He rose and quickly set about preparing the horses. He'd never seen anything like it.

## Chapter 4

*Your teacher may not exist but is real to you all the same. That matters.*

❧

Kellin was a town of several hundred people. It had grown up around the shores of the Black Lake, at the mouth of the River Meckle which drained it. The westernmost shore of the lake nestled at the base of the northern highlands – long low foothills eventually giving way to majestic snow-dusted mountains. Carg drove into the town to find lodgings at the tavern.

They thanked Carg for the ride as they shook hands. Wode looked Carg in the eye as he matched the muscular grip. "You'll get a better price for your hides than before."

It took a moment for Carg to pick up Wode's meaning and to his departing back he shouted, "Thank you, Wode," and got a waved response. "Not such an awkward cuss after all," he chuckled, and sure enough, when it came to market the buyers seemed to think his hides a better quality than last time.

"Where are we going to stay, Wode?"

"I have an old friend who is hopefully still with us." Wode led the way across the main street and turned down a road heading south. After a further left and right, he pushed open a gate in front of a small cottage. He looked up at the smoke rising from the chimney and knocked at the door. An old woman's voice called out from inside, "Who is it?"

"Wode of Brennan."

"WODE?" There was the sound of a chair moving and footsteps. The door was opened by an unusually tall woman in her autumn years. Her face lit up and she took Wode in a fond embrace.

"It is good to see you, young man," she said, standing back to examine him more closely. He met her gaze and didn't shy away from her assessment.

"You have been carrying great sadness, great pain." She paused. "Is it Mara?" she asked softly.

"She died in childbirth."

"Oh Wode. Oh Wode. Is there a tougher call on a man? And you would have done all in your power to save them." He nodded, trying to prevent his eyes moistening, and she hugged him again. Wode was silent as she stepped back, holding him at arm's length. Then she caught sight of Geeter. "Who's this?" she enquired, looking up at Wode.

"Geeter. We're on our way to Tulkney to see his mother." He turned to Geeter.

"Geeter, this is Mairhi, sister of the blessed Worian who I was apprenticed to."

Geeter stepped forward to shake her hand with the deference that Brackan youth traditionally held for their elders. Wode smiled approvingly: in Bracka, elders were held in respect for their wisdom, experience and their contribution to those who followed; the next generations walked the roads made, lived in the homes built and enjoyed the inventions of those who had gone before.

Mairhi had many more questions but merely said, "Come in, Geeter. We'll find you some supper."

---

Tired after the warm food, Geeter settled down beside the kitchen fire and was soon asleep, curled up on a reed mat under his father's old blanket.

Mairhi and Wode sat at the table, catching up on each other's lives. There was an easiness between them, oiled by enduring love and respect. She had been like a favourite aunt to him as he grew in knowledge over the years under her brother's tutelage. She was a gifted seer in her own right and many consulted her moresight for guidance on a wide range of matters, but predominantly those of love and family.

"Bring me up to date," she said quietly, her compassion reaching out to him.

Wode talked of the struggle to keep Mara alive during the long and arduous labour. She had been exhausted from hours of straining – the baby's head was large and just would not emerge – and she was bleeding internally. He talked of his frantic efforts and eventual powerlessness: a man who could do so many extraordinary things could not save his woman in the hour of her greatest need.

For the first time, he revealed the depths of his despair and helplessness at not being able to change the course of events; how he had turned inwards, found himself walking the lonely cliff-top path above the fathomless chasm of grief; and how he had doubted himself and his gifts – a gnoseer was not supposed to have such emotions. His talents did not desert him, but he was aware that his inner state was affecting the outcomes of those he helped. Such was his reputation and the depth of his gift that only he noticed. But that was all it took to sow the seed of self-doubt – that most undermining of human feelings. He spoke of it all: how he had acknowledged to himself that the purity of his work was being tainted and could become karmic, and that something had to be done. He had contemplated a solrom, he told her, with a mixture of foreboding and relief; the fear of facing the claw of his loneliness and the relief of being away from the touchstone reminders, as well as the well-meant sympathy of friends that fell short of his heart.

"How are you doing?"

"My perspective is better. The distance without has given me the space within to see the shadow of my emotion and its karma, and the passage of time has given me a higher view of the events, to remove self-blame. Almost. And he…" nodding in the direction of the sleeping figure by the fire, "has provided me with the opportunity to give of myself, to put my attention outside me."

"How did you come by the lad?"

Mairhi saw Wode smile as he recounted the events of recent days. "He is a bit tricky at times. His mother could have helped him more after the death of his father but he has talent, Mairhi: a great gift with birds. If it sits well with you, I would like to stay a few days and develop that magic within him so he has a real taste before we meet up with his mother."

"You could influence his mother's decision more easily," Mairhi said tentatively.

"I know, but that would not be right."

"Good for you, Wodey, always a stickler for the truth."

"'Wodey', I've not heard that in a long time."

Wode told Mairhi of Geeter's attempts to steal an egg, of their stay at Thrum and Keela's farm, and of Geeter's life with Sintle and his mother. "His father taught him well – he has done a great job of looking out for himself, and you know how important self-reliance is."

Mairhi nodded. It was all very well being gifted with moresight but its effect was to separate you from "normal" people. She had long ago learnt that a degree of separation was necessary in order to be objective in her work. Not that it was a conscious move on her part – ordinary folk became that little bit distant with seers and gnoseers – which was understandable, as everyone wanted to keep their innermost thoughts private and unread.

Wode changed the subject. "Have you heard of a farmer called Berlen? He's somewhere near Teksel, off the Kellin road. A widower."

"No, why?"

"He is Thrum's brother. According to Thrum, he started feeling ill several moon-cycles ago and his condition has been slowly deteriorating since. The herbalist is nonplussed as to the cause and cure. Thrum and Keela think there is sorcery behind it. They asked me to drop by and see what I could do. It's not a big detour from our way to Tulkney."

"I shall ask in the market tomorrow. Now it is time for this grey head to rest on its pillow. Will you be all right on the floor here?"

"Yes, thank you, Mairhi. Goodnight."

She got up and kissed him on the forehead.

--------------------

The next morning they crossed the river and walked a short distance into the hills away from the relative bustle of the town. Wode had said little on the way apart from that they were going to work with birds. Worian had shown him how important it was not to say too much: "To achieve something in life, you first must expect it of yourself. To give too much detail can provide ground for doubt to roam and spoil the burgeoning growth of talent." Wode had kept these words to heart over the years; and many a gnoseer had a story to tell of enthusiastic apprentices who moved mountains because they didn't know they couldn't.

"Right, this looks a good place." He laid down his staff and pack, and sat down. "I probably know the answer but tell me, Geeter, do you have a favourite bird?"

Geeter thought a moment. "I like all birds, but a predator has more power…probably a kite, a black kite."

"Good choice. Versatile and common enough. Come and sit in front of me." Geeter dropped his pack beside Wode's and sat down.

"What characteristics of the kite do you like?"

"Their effortless flight, their ability to swoop and turn tightly on a point." Geeter thought some more and continued, "The way they soar up high and the way they look about, seeing everything."

Wode narrowed his eyes. A perfect choice, he thought.

"All right, Geeter, now we are going to have some fun. Listen to me carefully." Geeter nodded expectantly.

"Close your eyes. Take some deep breaths…Relax, that's it. Keep breathing deeply." Wode moved his hands over the space surrounding Geeter, opening invisible gates in space. Geeter sighed.

Wode spoke slowly and sonorously: "Notice the lightness in you…how light can you be…feel…You are feeling lighter and lighter…weightless…light and effortless… You turn to face into the wind…You are feeling light – as though you are weightless…rising…Find yourself rising up now…into the sky…the ground is moving…further away…beneath you…You can see your body…seated below you…You feel full of energy…and power…as you look around…You smile…You want to move to your left and without effort you are heading left…That was easy, wasn't it? Now to go right…And you find you are moving over the ground to your right…up…down… It's all so easy…effortless. You are flying…You can see for miles…incredible detail…Higher and higher…down to your left…up to your right…. Swooping…diving… climbing high…circling on warm air…rising….You are Being in flight…"

Geeter had a smile of wonder from ear to ear – joy beaming out of him like a hilltop beacon.

"You look over to your left…down your wing and there is another in flight beside you…And you start to play…wide sweeping turns…chasing each other…and then you level up…You think, I'm going to fly up, and your companion immediately moves with you…And then you think, I'm going to fly to the right…and again your companion does the same immediately…And now you stay flying level and 'think' your companion to move left…and right…swoop down…and now climb high…towards the clouds…And your companion does everything you think to them…"

Wode was silent for some time, watching as Geeter's body gently swayed with the images within.

"And now it's time for you to land…and you thank them for playing with you today…and you ask them if they will do it again...'Yes,' they say, 'just call my name and I'll come to you.' 'Thank you,' you say, 'I'll see you soon,' and you descend gracefully...effortlessly...taking your time...and you land right here..." Wode waited a moment. "What was your companion's name, Geeter?"

Still with his eyes closed, "Keekra."

"And is that her up there?"

Geeter, blinking out of the depths of himself, opened his eyes to see Wode pointing to a kite circling above.

Geeter's jaw dropped in total shock. He felt his chest burst outwards as a wellspring of joy overflowed his body. Finally speech returned. "Keekra," he whispered and he heard the characteristic high-pitched gree-er si-si-si-si-si as she answered him.

Wode watched his young friend take it all in, remembering how he himself had felt the first time. It was a mind-shattering experience to realise that you had just flown as a bird. To have felt the wind coursing over your feathered wings, the effortless soaring up high and the sheer excitement of dropping down through the air, gathering speed from only the slightest flick of a wing.

"Wode..." Geeter was lost for words.

"Well done, Geeter. You are a flyer of some skill already. I'm going to leave you to practise now. Can you find your way back to Mairhi's house?"

Geeter nodded, not really hearing him.

"Good. Stay out here and practise your flying with Keekra. You have chosen each other. Fly over the town, have a look at people from the air, follow them. Have fun with it, feel it. Talk to her, let her get used to you. But remember to leave enough time for Keekra to get home before dark."

Geeter nodded again.

Wode got up, shouldered his pack, smiled down at the still-dumbfounded Geeter and left him to it.

———————

Wode had Geeter practise his flying often over the next few days, and not just with Keekra. He encouraged him to try flying solo over different parts of the town and countryside. On the second afternoon, Wode said, "Right, Geeter, I am going out and I want you to follow me from above and tell me what you see."

Geeter settled down, took some deep breaths and Wode closed the door softly behind him. He took in some easy landmarks: the lake, the town square, the big meeting house, then headed out on the road west, and east. He sat still for half an hour and even ran for a bit along the western road. He might have looked a bit odd going this way and that but gnoseers had a way of blending in, such that they disappeared to outside eyes. It was exhausting for longer than about twenty minutes, as it required immense concentration to change their emanation to that of their surroundings and thus blend in. He made sure he was invisible enough to go unnoticed at ground level but not so much to make it too difficult for Geeter.

When he returned Geeter was sitting exactly as he'd left him, eyes still closed. Wode poured them both some water and sat down. Geeter opened his eyes. He looked tired.

"Good control, Geeter, well done. Now, tell me what you saw."

"I saw you go by a lake, and a busy place with lots of people."

"That's good," Wode said encouragingly. "There is a lake and I went to the town square where the market is. What else?"

"Well, I thought I saw you and then I didn't and then I did. And at one point you seemed to stop for ages and then go off quite fast in the opposite direction."

"Very good. That's what I did. Well done."

Mairhi came in from the back carrying vegetables.

"Hello. What have you two been up to?"

"Wode's been out and I've been following by flying," said Geeter proudly.

"Have you indeed?" Mairhi turned to Wode. "I remember when Worian was teaching the same to you."

She smiled encouragingly at Geeter. "What's your preferred bird?"

"Black kite."

"Good choice, plenty of those about. Wode here went for the golden eagle and you have to wait a few minutes for them to arrive, don't you, Wode?"

Wode smiled. "But they are worth the wait."

"And then you started being lynx." She turned to Geeter. "Very few can manage a lynx, young man. To align your mind to such a magnificent animal takes a lot of presence, and you can't be distracted by emotions – worries or fears. Being wolf is easier and most leave it there." Turning to Wode, "That is why Worian loved you so much: you and he could go off into the forest together as lynx."

Geeter had been feeling very pleased with himself. Mairhi had seen this, and knowing that over-confidence can lead to mistakes, had chosen to gently remind him who was his teacher.

"Thank you, Mairhi." Wode understood. "Now, lad, let's help make supper."

The three of them worked well together; she allowed the boys to do most of the work as it wasn't every day that she had help. They were soon sitting down to a lovely supper.

"You are off tomorrow, aren't you?" Mairhi could sense this was the case and Wode confirmed it with a nod.

"Be wary of the woman." Wode raised his eyebrows and nodded again, and Geeter looked from one to the other.

"What woman? My mother?"

"No. I didn't tell you, Geeter, but Thrum asked me to drop in at his brother's farm. He is worried about him.

He has been sick awhile and the cures are not working."

"But what about my…" Geeter started impatiently, and then stopped himself. "Well, is it far?"

"No, a day and a half. Not that you are in any hurry to see old Sintle again." Wode couldn't resist a little dig and Geeter wrinkled his nose in disgust.

"What do you see for me, Mairhi?" Geeter ventured hopefully.

She looked at Wode, who nodded imperceptibly. "You and your mother have a decision to make. It is not one she is expecting as she has not been paying close enough attention these past few years. The man could make it easy for you both."

"Wode?"

"He who stands beside your mother."

"Oh, that's Sintle." Geeter looked crestfallen.

"It will be all right, Geeter. Don't worry. Spirit knows what you need and it will be given."

Geeter brightened. "Thank you, Mairhi."

"And you, Wode, don't let them know you are a gnoseer." Mairhi thought for a second. "Just tell them you are a carpenter, like your father. And this one is your apprentice." She gestured towards Geeter. "And watch your back," she said to Wode. "Your 'preoccupation' could be a distraction."

*Chapter 5*

*The Truth requires no energy to sustain it.*
*It just is.*

Teksel was a large village with small-town aspirations. Situated a day's ride from Kellin down the Kuik road, or nearly two days of steady walking, it boasted a large tavern, a blacksmith and several stalls of good country fare. Wode and Geeter's progress had been slow as no carts or wagons had come their way and huge thunderstorms had made the road heavy-going.

Wode loved thunder and lightning, nature's most awe-inspiring and magnificent of shows: the air full of a vibrant vitality as though the universe were pouring energy into the world and the more it poured, the more nature's space opened up her cup; the rolling walls of booming sound excited every cell in his body and if he was able he'd venture into a downpour and take a rain bath accompanied by booming thunder and flashing fingers of fire. During one spectacular storm, they were sheltering by a warm fire under a huge oak and to Geeter's utter astonishment his hitherto rather serious companion dropped his clothing in a pile and ran out into the watery deluge to play with the elements. Geeter caught the spirit of the moment and stripped off too, sprinting out into the middle of the bright green pastureland to join him. Shouting and dancing, they cantered around the meadow in wild abandon, like uncaged lunatic monkeys tasting first freedom. Laughing and breathless, Wode stopped, vigorously scrubbed his skin with a large ball of grass until he glowed and then stood with arms out wide, face to the heavens, gratefully letting the cold rain wash over him, taking with it the grass, the dirt and the past. Geeter, not taken to such fastidiousness, merely carried on careering around the meadow until he collapsed in a sodden, happy, panting heap.

As the exhilaration left them, they retreated to the fire to dry off. "Mad, eh?" Wode grinned. "The energy of Life is like the wind, you can feel its effect but you never know where it is going to take you!"

"I love big storms too, but I never thought to do that!" Geeter grinned back.

———

With tired bodies and stomachs rumbling like distant thunder, they made their way to the town tavern. No one paid any attention as they entered the warm fuggy atmosphere of ale-infused bonhomie and made their way to the back of the main room. The food came quickly and they wolfed it down. As they sat with their supper settling, Wode asked the mistress of the house about Berlen.

"Oooh, let me see. Berlen's place is just east of here, about two hours' walk. If you take the road by the smithy's you'll get there. He's not been himself of late: memory's gone to pot and he's seeing funny too. Remembers the old days but not the new. Some say he's gone to drink but he's not that way, always was careful when he came to town, even after a good market in Kellin. Did you know his wife?" Wode shook his head.

"He took ol' Fabrayer's death hard, and I know he's had run-ins with his boy and daughter-in-law 'bout how the farm should be run." She warmed to her theme. "Yes, that bloody Palt, comes back from five years in a town and reckons he's a better farmer than his father. He was such a nice boy. Could be his missus, mind, never looks me in the eye but you can't hold that against anyone, can ye?"

"No," Wode agreed. "And can you tell me the name of a good carpenter in these parts?"

"Turb, I reckon is the best. He's a goodun." And with that she was off pouring ale into thirsty cups.

"We'll go there tomorrow, Geeter, and see what we shall see." Wode downed his cup and stood up to lead the way to bed. He felt uneasy, but he couldn't quite place why. The ale had distorted his perception and he knew it. He took extra care with his night-time routine.

---

The following day was fine and warm, large clouds slowly forming shapes for the travellers' entertainment; as they strode along Geeter was happily pointing out white fluffy figures forming and fading – cows and fish and all manner of outlandish monsters. Wode as usual was more preoccupied with what plants were growing, as this was just north of the fertile Tulrain basin.

"Wode?"

"Mmm?"

"If we choose our life, why do some folk choose to be crippled?"

"Now that," said Wode, "is a good question." He paused thoughtfully. "Tell me, Geeter, have you ever struggled to carry something and then a stronger man or woman came to take your burden from you?"

"Er yes, I suppose so...When we were loading the wagons to move to Tulkney after Father died, we were helped by Tolo – a big strong man who used to help Father with the farm. He saw me struggling with a box and he just came up, tapped me on the shoulder and took it out of my hands, easy as anything."

"And you know how we always look after the sick and elderly if we can?"

"Yes."

"Well it's a bit like that really. Do you remember we spoke about karma?" Geeter nodded. "Well not many people know this, but the object of living a life is to die without any shadow of negative emotion – jealousy, anger, fear, resentment − left in you. Leave with a clean slate, just as you entered. If we are aware enough to pick up the signs, Life is our teacher. Most people are looking for happiness outside themselves, where they won't find it, and if they think they have, it won't last. The secret to Life is to be free of any unhappiness within, so that you are in contact with the amazing Spirit that you truly are. And if you act from there in the world, you will be in harmony with nature and the universe, and your life will be simple, powerful and magical. The Great Spirit will support you and good things will happen more and more."

They walked in silence awhile, Geeter pondering the gnoseer's words.

"But," Geeter finally said, "how does this explain why someone would want to be a cripple?"

"Well, most people do not die free of negative emotion, with a clean slate. This unhappiness they have not let go of remains as part of the emotional energy that hangs around the earth, like an invisible dark cloud, and it causes difficulties for the generations yet to come. I remember being angry with someone once − they'd falsely accused me of something − and then all of a sudden, whooom, this huge surge of anger came into me, a rage really. I was dumbfounded; it wasn't mine.

So where had it come from? I was learning about energy at the time with Worian, and he told me about the energetic or emotional bridges we build into the dark shadowy clouds of emotion that hang around the earth, and how black energy can travel across them into us. He showed me that if we are sad we will attract sadness to us, and if we are resentful we will attract the dark energy of resentment into us, left by previous generations hanging around the earth."

"That doesn't sound very nice."

"No, it's not," Wode agreed. "Now, to answer your question: we all take on a portion of this dark emotional energy at birth as our karma and it plays out as the circumstances of our life. As a service to us all, beautiful old souls volunteer to take on more of the portion of this karma in their next life and this burden comes in the form of illness or disability. And when they do so, some of the emotional energy that hangs around the earth is slightly reduced. So this is another reason why we look after the sick and crippled, as gratitude for their taking on a bigger burden on behalf of us all."

"For a soul to volunteer for that is..." Geeter gulped, lost for words.

"Yes, it is." They continued in silence for a while.

"Is that why Thrum's brother Berlen is sick?"

"It is possibly by design. But I doubt it is of his choosing."

Geeter wasn't entirely sure what Wode was implying, but he sensed that the subject was closed and they continued on in companionable silence. Before long they came across a man leading a donkey loaded up with wood.

"Greetings," hailed Wode.

"Likewise, sir."

"Is Berlen's property nearby?"

"Aye, just over this rise here – you'll see the orchards beside the farmstead."

Wode thanked the man and they quickened their pace. From the top of the hill they could see the orchards and an attractive, well-proportioned house with smoke being teased out of the chimney by a light breeze.

"Remember now, I am your uncle Orlech. We don't want them to know I am a gnoseer, nor that you are a runaway." Geeter nodded and Wode could almost see his heart beating faster with the ruse of it all.

They strolled down the slope and up to the house. Wode stood in front of the door and closed his eyes a moment, then knocked firmly. And knocked again. There was a sound of footsteps to the left of them and they turned to see a handsome blonde woman with high cheekbones come round the corner with a handful of pegs.

"Yes?"

"Greetings, you must be Rekle. My name is Orlech and this is Geeter. I'm a friend of Thrum, Berlen's brother. We are on our way to Kuik. Thrum asked me to visit, to pass on his news and good wishes."

"Oh, yes." Wode saw a shadow pass across her eyes.

"Can we help with the washing?"

"Er no…thank you." Rekle was caught on the hop but regained her wits. "Berlen is inside. Won't you come in for a drink and…" She paused for a second. "It's lunch soon. You must join us."

"Thank you. You are kind."

Brackan hospitality dictated that you took in travellers for at least a meal, so it was no less than they expected. Wode was grateful for this ancient custom, and over the years had enjoyed countless meals in many households. He too had fed travellers who brought news, entertainment and skills that could be put to good use. Some did literally sing for their supper.

Rekle led them into a large, untidy kitchen and sat them down at an old worn oak table with stools. Wode asked for water and Geeter was given some milk.

"Thrum tells me you came to live here after Fabrayer died."

"Yes, well, with no other children to help around the family farm it seemed we had no choice."

"Did you mind – you're from the town, aren't you?"

Rekle shot Wode a glance but saw only a blank half-smile. "No, not at all, we were ready to move and Palt has always wanted to come back to the farm."

"Oh, that's good. Why did he leave in the first place?"

"Oh, to get some life experience I think, find a wife."

Thrum had said that Palt was good with money and had done well as a merchant's assistant.

"I'll go and find Berlen and tell him he's got visitors. He's not been well but he's having a good day today."

"Is it bad?" Wode asked.

"Well, he can get a little irritable, and his memory deserts him sometimes. He sees things – not like a seer – and sometimes he vomits and gets the browns."

"Oh, poor fellow," said Wode sympathetically.

"Yes, and the herbalist is at a loss…" And with that Rekle left the room.

Geeter got up and walked over to the cat, which was in a prime position beside the fire. After some tickling behind the ear they were firm friends and Geeter settled down with her on his lap.

Rekle was back. "He's just coming. Now, I'd better get some food prepared."

Geeter looked at Wode, who nodded. "Can I give you a hand?"

"Thank you, Geeter. Yes, you can put this on the fire and stir it so it doesn't burn on the bottom," and Rekle handed him a large wooden spoon. "It's unusual to get such an offer from a young man."

"My father died a couple of years ago, and my mother liked the help and company in the kitchen." Geeter was aware of Wode's cautionary glance but carried on unconcerned.

"We tried the farm without him but it wasn't the same, and before long we sold it and moved into Tulkney. I didn't like living in the town and so my mother thought it would be good for me to spend some time with Uncle Orlech and perhaps learn to be a carpenter."

Wode smiled inwardly at Geeter's story-weaving. And coming from a boy, all the more believable. Clever lad, he thought. Just don't get carried away.

In walked a man looking pale and drawn. He was unsteady on his feet.

"Ah Berlen, this is Geeter and his uncle Orlech."

As the three greeted each other, Wode was instinctively assessing Berlen's energy field and could see his illness was centred on his right-hand side, just beneath the ribs. Berlen looked to see where to sit and the rapid turning of his head made him unsteady. Wode was up in a flash to steady him before he fell, and guided him to a seat. As he helped Berlen down into the chair he quickly moved his hand down his right flank and saw Berlen wince with the pressure over his liver. Wode tucked the clue away.

"How long need I stir this?" Geeter regained the attention.

"Just keep going." Rekle brought over a cup of water and placed it beside Berlen's left hand. Wode felt Berlen's energy change: animosity.

"Thrum says old Kettle is doing well." Wode delivered the password.

Berlen looked up gratefully. "I'm very glad to hear of the old girl." Berlen acknowledged the old Brackan custom – for when a traveller was sent to visit by another member of the family, the traveller was given a password to include in early conversation to authenticate his or her story.

"Were you born here, Berlen?"

"No, in Athale. Thrum got the farm there and I married Fabrayer. We lived here with her parents until they died." Berlen seemed quite gruff. Wode assumed his sickness was not helping his mood.

"Have you got many head?"

"Yes, a couple of hundred. Golden chilluns." Wode whistled under his breath. These cattle were renowned for being difficult to rear, but their milk and meat were highly prized above all other cattles and so was their value. Berlen was a wealthy man.

They continued to make small talk until the meal was ready and Wode said, "If you are up to it, I'd like you to show me round your land."

"Indeed I will, and if you are in no hurry, stay a night or so. I have been ill, and we rarely have visitors, so I would be glad of some fresh company."

"Thank you, Berlen. A night or two would be nice, eh Geeter?" Wode caught Rekle's frown out of the corner of his eye.

There was an awkward pause, which was interrupted when a tall man about Rekle's age strode into the kitchen. Wode and Geeter both stood respectfully. "You must be Palt," said Wode, offering his hand. Wode took in the high forehead, long nose and stubborn jaw as Rekle explained who they were.

"And your father has asked them to stay a night or so."

"That's nice," Palt said, ignoring his wife's look. "I'm sure they will be good company and a helping hand is always welcome," and with that, they all sat down to eat, polite conversation flowing back and forth.

---

Geeter and Wode joined Berlen on horseback for a tour of the farm. The farmer rode slowly so they took their time looking out across what they could see of Berlen's land from the hills. The old man became quite talkative as he warmed to his two companions; he was pleased to hear about Thrum, Keela and the boys, and reminisced about growing up with his younger brother Thrum. Wode bided his time before steering him round to the present and asking about his illness.

"I get these terrible headaches, and feel so ill. It's strange. Folk have said it's a reaction to my wife Fabrayer's death but I was at peace with it."

"Have you felt her presence since?"

"Oh yes. Not so much now – it is difficult for her to reach me when I'm feeling sick. But I know she's complete."

"That is good."

Berlen made no mention of the foul play that Thrum suspected, so Wode probed a little further: "And you are taking herbs?"

"A woman from Teksel comes out every half-moon."

"And she prepares your remedies?"

"She leaves a bundle of herbs – foul stuff, looks like the forest floor scraped into a gathering cloth. She gave Rekle instructions for its preparation. Rekle does it all. I just drink the foul-tasting brew she gives me."

Wode ceased his questions for a while as Berlen pointed out the perimeters of his land; good fertile soil with large golden cattle dotted about. Geeter was only half paying attention as he was more interested in watching an osprey hunt a large lake beneath the hill on which they stood.

"Look at that big fish. He can't get out of the water!" They all watched the osprey thrashing the air above the water as it tried to lift off with a pike. The fish was writhing about, making things difficult for its captor. Eventually it weakened and the osprey was able to slowly gain height.

"Well done," Geeter called out.

Berlen chuckled and shook his head. "I could have sworn I heard the bird reply!"

There was a silence as they watched the osprey. Weighed down by its family's next meal, it was working hard to gain altitude. Wode broke their reverie. "Presumably you will leave the farm to Palt?"

Berlen sighed. "We had no other children, so yes. But Palt never showed much interest in farming until recently. I'm not convinced it's really what he wants. He was doing well in Kuik as a merchant's assistant in one of the better trading houses. He's good with money...I don't know," he sighed. "Palt would probably just sell the farm and go back to the town."

"Does that trouble you?"

"Land, Orlech. It's the most important thing there is after family. Thrum's boys enjoy the farming life so I've thought about passing some of the land to them. But Palt's here now...Well, when I'm gone, which doesn't seem so far away now, it won't trouble me, will it? I'll be elsewhere."

"Give it to the boys," said Geeter ruefully under his breath.

--------------

That evening Wode and Geeter yawned through supper and went to bed soon after they had finished. As they settled down, Wode said, "You did well today, Geeter. Gave a good story and then kept your silence too."

"Thanks, Wode."

"Orlech!"

"Sorry. Orlech...That osprey was a wonderful sight, wasn't it?"

"Mmm," agreed Wode and set about his nightly routine: raising his hands above his head and stroking them down all around several times.

"I've seen you do this before," Geeter said, imitating Wode and his arm movement. "What are you doing?"

Wode chuckled at Geeter's parody. "Sitting invisibly above everyone's head is an orb of golden light. It is a source of energy and a gateway to the spirit world. I reach up into its middle and pull the light down around me like a protective cloak or shield; it is called a shieldagh. It is for when my guard is down during sleep; it prevents me from being attacked in the night."

"Attacked? By what?" A floorboard creaked outside their room. They both froze like statues, their ears straining to the furthest reaches of hearing, to the space before silence.

"Someone's been listening to us," Geeter whispered.

Wode sighed and lowered his voice. "Oh dear, they will know that was gnoseer talk. But we cannot be sure they heard anything, so we will just behave as normal."

Wode moved soundlessly to the door and listened to the hallway, scanning his senses. "Nobody there, not now anyway," he whispered as he settled back down. "Anyway, to answer your question, the energy cloak is to prevent attack from black magic – sorcery. The difference between black and white magic is the intent of the person doing it. If someone intends to cause another harm and they are well practised in the energy arts, they can. In the opposite way, gnoseers always intend to do good, and so they do."

"Should I do the same?" Geeter gestured with his arms above his head.

"It won't do you any harm." Smiling, Geeter made elaborate movements to pull down his own energy cloak around him, immediately noticing a delightful sense of calm.

"And do not forget to push it back up in the morning. Otherwise you will tire yourself out. Goodnight, Geeter."

"Goodnight, Orlech."

"Geeter." Wode was shaking him gently to wake up.

"Uuuuurhm?"

"Geeter, I have to go."

"Where?"

"I have been called to the Wisdom Tree."

Geeter was rubbing his eyes. "How?" He was interested, and eager to learn.

"It comes to me in a dream, an intuition, and then there's a pulling in my chest which only goes away when I get to the Tree."

Geeter hesitated, sensing what the answer would be, but he asked anyway. "Can I come?"

"No." Wode paused. "You are staying here."

"I want to go to the Wisdom Tree. I want to know my destiny," Geeter wailed.

"And I need you to stay here to keep an eye on things," Wode replied sternly.

"Why?" Defiance was beginning to seduce Geeter.

"Because someone is poisoning Berlen." Geeter's jaw dropped.

Wode took advantage of having Geeter's full attention and continued with his plan. "According to Berlen, Rekle is the one giving him his medicine. I need you here to watch where Rekle goes, what she does – and to see if she picks any plants. It is most important. Follow her as bird if she goes off by herself." Geeter nodded. "That way she won't suspect. And at other times, stick by Berlen. I expect he is safer with one of us around."

Geeter nodded, seemingly enjoying the trust placed in him. "I see it is essential I stay with him," he said with youthful self-importance.

"Good lad." Wode patted him on the shoulder. "And watch Palt too; his heart is not clear at the moment either."

Geeter nodded. "But what will you tell them as to why you are leaving me behind?"

"I will have a word with Berlen and explain I had promised to help out the carpenter in Teksel for a few days, and that I need the money for our travels. I will tell him you need a bit of a break from the road and ask if he would mind if you stayed. He seems to have taken a bit of a shine to you, so I know he will be glad of your company."

"All right, Wode."

"Orlech!"

"Orlech."

"Right, return your shieldagh up to the source and let's go down for breakfast."

## Chapter 6

*Your joy is You and is immeasurable.*

∽∽

Wode crested the rise and stopped to look down on the wide Tulrain plain, a green fertile valley of nature's abundance – as far as the eye could see, lush grasslands edged with tall forests of fir, beech and oak. He loved this view and sat down to rest his eyes on its soft horizons and trace the line of the great Tulrain River meandering its way south.

He'd been walking hard for two days and if he relaxed his eyes he could just make out the Wisdom Tree – Bracka's heart. It stood apart from a grove of large trees, but the Tree of Knowledge was bigger still and dwarfed those around it like a majestic emperor. It had seen its neighbours come and go over the centuries, and still it stood, unbowed by storm or the weight of time. Wode loved the Tree, and its presence was unlike anything else he'd known: during his apprenticeship to Worian, he had travelled to the four corners of Bracka to learn from the wisest gnoseers and even left the island's shores to travel in faraway lands. All gnoseers had favourite places – mountains, rivers, forests, sea – and used their gifts, combining the energy from these sites, but all loved the Tree above all. It was a rare place indeed, where myth and reality united to dance Life's great mystery; the air breathed under the Tree's branches was full of the bounty and promise of possibility; the crystal waters in the stream nearby appeared to float above the pebbles tracing its meandering course; and all around was a sense of peace, like a perfect sunrise – a dawn of stillness connecting all Life, the Oneness of being.

Rested, Wode could not wait any longer and set off again down the gentle escarpment and onto the vast expanse of the Tulrain grasses, lazily swishing like the pristine tails of coiffured thoroughbreds. He smiled at his sense of homecoming, a lightness of heart like a young lover's travelling to keep a prearranged romantic rendezvous; imperceptibly his pace quickened. As he walked, his thoughts of course turned to Geeter. 'He would love this journey,' he thought, acknowledging to himself that, despite what initially felt like an unwelcome intrusion, he did enjoy the boy's company. His eager intelligence brought out a sense of purpose in Wode that was adding new meaning to his life. Wode realised he enjoyed teaching him about Life and a gnoseer's ways, and Geeter's keen mind, dulled by emotion and neglect, eagerly soaked up knowledge like a flower basking in the sun's munificence. He had gifts, he listened well, and was open to the magical possibilities of destiny – a potential in all of us without the limitations of rigid thinking. Wode knew that it was within the realms of Geeter's karma that he apprentice him, but the key was his mother. There was still a card that needed to be laid down and she was the only one who could bring it into play.

Wode looked up to see a pair of plains eagles soaring in the sky. He reached into the mind of one, seeing out of its eyes – the vast distances and detail were breathtaking; a bird has senses most humans can only dream of. Wode was the happiest he had been for a long time. Through the eagle's eyes he could easily see the Wisdom Tree and one lone figure walking about underneath it. He had paced the ground around the Tree for many days himself, and he knew the nooks and crannies created by the web of immense roots feeding into the colossal trunk. There was one with lovely smooth sides beside which he often slept, snug in his blanket between it and an adjacent root branch. It did not afford much room to move and so he was often a bit stiff on waking, but the sheer deep comfort of being held in sleep by the Tree was more than worth the stiff muscles in the morning. People had often asked him what elders and gnoseers did for food, as sometimes they were there for several weeks. There was never a shortage; people coming to the Tree always brought gifts of food to those who gave them divination, and the grove nearby had fruit trees in abundance. There were also walnut trees, chestnut, hazel and a wide variety of fungi, but what gave new visitors the most surprise was the wild hens that scratched around the grove. No one knew how they came to be there – they had probably been brought by an enterprising gnoseer who liked his eggs – but they made good company and finding fresh eggs was always an enjoyable pastime. Everything was protected by the Tree, and so the hens weren't in danger from foxes or wolves and the cockerels ensured no one attending the Tree overslept!

In no time he was near enough to the Tree to see a figure come out from under its vast shade to stand and wave. Wode returned the wave, recognising an old friend from the furthest corner of Bracka who had for several moon-cycles taught him the laws of time. It was a lifetime of knowledge he had imparted to Wode – deep, vast secrets of the universe – too much to learn in such a short time, but the seeds of knowledge had been sown within him and Wode had watered and nurtured them every day since.

"Wode of Brennan!"

"Awken of Ballakuik!" he shouted back and quickened his pace.

Wode could see Awken had not changed a bit and embraced his well-fed, balding friend who only just made it up to his armpit. They laughed in the pleasure of greeting and friendship.

"You are looking as prosperous as ever," winkled Wode.

Awken patted his ample belly. "Well, with three women in my life, what do you expect? And you are…changed, but looking like coming back to your old self." Wode acknowledged his old friend's assessment.

"I heard about Mara," Awken said, shaking his head. "That was tough, very tough," and he patted Wode's arm sympathetically. "Karma, eh?" He sighed. He paused, letting an insight settle in him. "You are a better man for the experience and you will love again, and it will be even more unifying than before." He winked at Wode. "A happy thought indeed, no?"

Wode smiled and nodded. "Thank you, Awken."

"Come, let us share some food and catch up. I shall sleep after lunch and then head off to Kuik. There will be several hours of daylight for good walking this day."

⸻

Wode had spent the night in blissful comfort, enveloped by the roots and presence of the great Tree. He'd had some vivid dreams of Geeter and so he knew something was amiss, but he'd also had dream glimpses of a tall woman with long raven hair and beautiful, deep green eyes. He considered the dreams on waking, looking for their message. Seeing a woman so vividly had unsettled him because he wasn't used to the idea of being attracted to a female other than Mara. Was it just Awken's words playing on his loss? Or was she to be part of his future? Even for gnoseers, the contract with destiny could be largely shrouded — for if we knew it all before, we would not strive to unravel our destiny and learn the lessons hidden within a life: the refinement of experience into cosmic knowledge and wisdom — real alchemy. Nothing was clear to him, and finally he just stopped pondering on it and began the day.

Wode stretched the aches out of his body and then went to the stream to wash and drink, and clean some mushrooms and fruit he'd picked. He put some wood on "the fire that never went out" and with two eggs, made a mushroom mess in the bottom of a pot – one of several to choose from that had been left by various keepers over the years. He washed it all down with some tea – dried leaves tapped out from his leather pouch that never left him – and then set about cleaning the pot and tidying under the Tree.

The rest of the day was spent walking about, exploring what was new in the grove, talking to the chickens and any other animals that he saw, and meditating – stilling his mind in preparation for the divination he had been called to perform. With his mind suitably still, he also connected to Geeter to reassure him and protect him as much as he could: communicating in the inner realm was not an exact science and largely an ancient forgotten way. He remembered Worian telling him that, when people said a person was "in their thoughts", it was an unconscious recognition of a way of being from long ago, when we were all connected through the once pure inner realm, and words were rarely used. It was an important lesson as Worian then began to show him how gnoseers retained this ability to go within and connect to the earth, nature and people. From the outside it looked as though the gnoseer was asleep sitting upright, but inside they were travelling the subconscious and unconscious to seek answers and insights. "It can only be done in stillness," Worian had said. "Movement and talking in the conscious realm is like splashing in the shallows, we must dive deep where ideas are pure embryonic energy, awaiting the light of intelligence to become thought, emotion and concept." Wode smiled at the memory of his old teacher.

Wode also spent time tracking Palt and Rekle in the inner realm. What he saw didn't please him, but his internal roaming was cut short by the gentle clopping of hooves in the distance and he turned to see two riders leading a packhorse coming towards him from the direction of Kuik. He knew immediately that these two were his reason for being called to the Tree.

He sat and watched them approach, tuning into their energy. Both sat tall in the saddle − an older man and a younger woman − wearing fine-looking clothes and riding strong, beautiful horses. These were plains horses with long legs for speed through tall grass. Wode was more used to seeing highland stock − shorter in leg and built for hard-going on uneven highland terrain. They were obviously townsfolk and he sensed they were father and daughter. She was the questioner.

As they drew near and dismounted, Wode stood to greet them. The father spoke. "Greetings, revered friend."

"And a warm welcome to you both. My name is Wode of Brennan." The woman took a sharp intake of breath.

"Are you all right?" His name rarely caused mild shock.

"Yes, yes," she said. "It's just that I was told by a seer friend the Keeper would be from the north highlands… and it's true."

"You doubted it?" he challenged playfully.

"Well, I'm not used to the company of gnoseers. I mean no disrespect but there are ways in the town that we do not honour enough."

Wode warmed to her courtesy and noted her long black hair – he was reminded of the woman in his dream; her large eyes looked blue but her face was in shadow so he could not be sure. He smiled. "I was not being serious but thank you for your kind words. May I know your names?"

"Oh sorry, yes. This is my father, Harrell, and I am Deera."

Wode bowed slightly theatrically, surprising himself.

Harrell had been watching their exchange with a smile. He was used to men responding to his daughter in this way; she wasn't the most beautiful woman in Kuik but there was a grace and loveliness about her which could make grown men easily forget themselves. He had doubted their reason for coming but, when someone was called to the Wisdom Tree, they must travel. The exchange that took place was not just for the questioner's benefit: ancient lore had it that the words spoken in answer to the question benefited all humanity. The question arising in someone was part of the karmic cleansing of the collective self, and such was the power of the Tree that the answer was a healing response to be emanated back into the collective inner realm.

"Are you equipped for a night away? It's just that it is a full moon tonight and therefore tomorrow is a better time for new beginnings. It all depends on your question."

"We are prepared for more than a night. That would suit us very well."

"I will help you with the horses. Afterwards you can walk off any riding stiffness and then we can eat before dark."

Wode helped Harrell unsaddle the horses and they immediately dropped their heads to feed. Wode lifted the head of Deera's horse and walked her to the stream with Harrell following his lead.

"You've come from Kuik?"

Harrell sensed Wode already knew the answer. "Yes, we set off early this morning. I've not had a good hack for as long as I can remember. I'm a bit wobbly on my legs," he laughed.

"I think I would be too," Wode conceded. "Is Deera your only daughter?"

"Yes, but Aruna and I have also been blessed with a son. He works with me and will take over one day. I trade in cloth, wool mainly."

Wode was interested to know more. "And is trade good?"

"Yes, very. I work hard but it is something that seems to come easily to me. My only grumble would be the frequent travel overseas, as I'm sometimes away up to half a year at a time."

"Yes, being away from loved ones is often hard."

"Yes. It's harder for Aruna as sometimes my son and I are away together; but he has to meet my customers and I console myself that she has Deera."

Wode nodded. "Life's a balance that few get right within them." The horses, having drunk their fill, were now pulling at the grass on the stream's edges. Wode tugged at the reins he was holding. "Come on, you, I need to get some supper for my guests." And with that he started up the slope towards the Tree.

---

They spent the evening talking like old friends, as was often the case under the Tree. Wode had made them a simple supper with Deera's help, and whilst washing vegetables by the stream he'd found himself telling her about the death of Mara and his son. She had said nothing but her eyes told him she understood, she knew similar pain.

"It is the hard experiences that really shape us," she said.

"Yes...that is true."

"I was to be wed to a lovely man called Beam. His family are old friends, and he was like another son to my father.

Three years ago he fell off a horse in the harvest festival race. Never before in the race's long history had someone died, but that year Beam came off when a strap broke on his saddle. He fell, hitting his head on a large stone, the only one for miles around…it was his destiny. And mine too." She was silent with the weight of the memory, of hopes extinguished in a moment. "I love him still."

"Do you still think of him?"

"Now and again."

"You mustn't," Wode said gently.

Deera turned her large green eyes and looked into his. "Why do you say that?"

"For your peace of mind."

"But I don't want to forget him."

"And you won't…but don't remember him."

"I…I don't understand."

"I speak from experience. Remembering is like touching an open sore. Every time we think of them it touches that mental soreness and it hurts. When we aren't thinking of them, we don't hurt. Your love for him is in your heart and not your mind. Love never dies. You will never be without him as he is here within you." He touched his chest to illustrate.

Deera thought for a moment. "I see: my mind is trying to hold on to something that does not exist outside my heart." She smiled at him with the dignity of an angel, whilst the new knowledge settled in her, healing her. "Thank you."

They said little as they finished washing the vegetables and then made their way back to the fire under the Tree. Wode was also aware of something having shifted in him. A subtle lightness in his chest from having shared a moment of grace with a woman he didn't know – but found he wanted to.

———————

They awoke the following morning and went about what people do first thing. Harrell and Deera watched Wode put his body through the stretches that he undertook most mornings to keep supple and strong. He then got some breakfast going with fruit and a porridge, and made some sweet tea from the flowers of the Wisdom Tree. He handed them their cups with an expectant smile. "You might not have tasted this before."

Intrigued, they both sipped the hot brew, delighting in its unique flavours. "It's wonderful," Deera said.

Wode smiled at her. "I suggest we address your question this morning. That will leave you plenty of time to make headway into your return to Kuik."

"Excellent," said Harrell.

They ate their porridge and fruit appreciatively, and then Deera went to wash the bowls and pots in the stream.

"I think Deera will put her tragedy more easily behind her now."

"Beam, you mean?" Wode nodded.

"That would be good; it hit her hard. He was a great fellow, full of laughter and fun. Wonderful company."

They heard Deera begin to sing an old traditional ballad down by the stream and they stopped to listen. She started back towards them, her soft lilting voice going before her.

> *For she is magnificent, all kindness and good*
> *And all admire her beauty.*
> *Many have tried to lighten her heart*
> *But none have reached her truly.*

> *Nobles and princes, the finest of men,*
> *Have journeyed to win her hand.*
> *With grace she receives them, hearing their tales,*
> *Of adventures in faraway lands.*

"She has a beautiful voice, Harrell. Does she get that from you?"

"I do like to fill the air with a song," Harrell replied, and with that he harmonised with Deera as she drew near. She smiled as she heard her father's notes combine with hers to dance the air like invisible faeries, a warm melodic fragrance wafting around grateful ears.

> *They come with treasures of jewel and cloth*
> *And some promise riches for ever,*
> *But she's not swayed by gifts or what's told –*
> *She's awaiting a true man's endeavour.*
>
> *Deep inside, a woman knows love –*
> *Her heart's own knowledge at birth.*
> *She'll outstay patience for him to arrive,*
> *For the one who knows her true worth.*
>
> *She's wise and knowing that Life will provide*
> *A love so heroic and strong.*

*She's the light in woman for ages to come –*
*The grace lighting hearts to go on.*

As Wode listened, he realised he was enjoying himself, a welcome lightness tickling his serious demeanour. The ballad tailed off into its meaningful silence, broken only by Wode clapping his appreciation.

"You both have beautiful voices."

"Thank you, kind sir," responded Deera. The song's magic began to fade, the notes receding into the vast nothing they came from.

Deera sighed. "Well if it's time, it's time," she said, looking at Wode.

"Yes. Give me a few minutes to prepare myself. I will be over there," he said, pointing to a huge well-worn root bench, "and when I signal come over and sit opposite me if you would." Deera nodded and sat down to wait.

Wode went to his chosen place and sat quietly with eyes closed. Breathing deeply, he called to the power of the Wisdom Tree beyond his mind and merged his energy with the Tree's. He felt a great stillness spread through him and he simply sat there with nothing in him. After a few minutes he opened his eyes and gestured Deera over, guiding her to a broad root branch worn smooth over the years from use. She settled herself comfortably and looked over at him in patient expectation.

He spread a thick woven cloth on the ground between them and then picked up a worn leather pouch about the size of his hand, out of which he poured twelve black shiny pebbles.

"Have you ever had the stones thrown for you before?"

Deera nodded. "Yes, once or twice, I think, with a seer."

Wode nodded. "Good. I like to start a divination with the stones as it can reveal helpful insights and knowledge in people, and it also helps the questioner to take their awareness deep into their inner realm – to the place of possible future.

"So just to remind you, I will throw the stones and tell you what I see. When I give you the reading, I am not interpreting it in any way. The information revealed is for you and you alone – the questioner. And it is in you that the answer or solution must be allowed to rise. You can ask me any questions you like, and my responses will guide you, but the answer needs to manifest in you, and it will. It may not come immediately – perhaps tomorrow, perhaps in the next days or even weeks. The images I see and report to you will have some form of clue or opening for you. Do not judge them, even if they sound ridiculous. If your mind discards any of the information, it may be blocking your answer."

"I understand, Wode."

He smiled across at Deera and gathered up the twelve small black pebbles and, cupping his hands, shook them whilst muttering an ancient mantra under his breath. He leaned towards Deera and held open his hands.

"Please focus on your question or problem, feel what it feels like and then blow that feeling into the stones." He waited until she had blown onto the pebbles in his hands and then dropped them onto the cloth beneath.

He looked at them for some moments and then said, "Pick one."

Deera studied them all and then reached out to an irregularly shaped one on her left. "Please place it in the centre of the cloth." She did as instructed and he gathered up the remaining stones and gave them to her to hold.

"Now, again hold the question in your mind and then blow into the stones from there."

Deera focused for a minute, gently blew onto the stones and then passed them back. Cupping them in his big hands, Wode clasped them to his chest, muttered a few words and then released them to find their position on the cloth. He looked down at the shiny black pebbles and then slowly began to read from the pattern of what he saw.

"I see a swan flying above a woman upon a horse...she's riding...beside a lake...in a valley with deep sides... There is a cloud passing over the sun." He waited but there was nothing more and he gathered up the stones. Again he clasped the pebbles to his chest, closed his eyes and released the stones for a second time.

"The cloud is less dense...there is more light...She is still riding, looking about her...as if searching for something...A swan is keeping her company. Some people...men, walk towards her and she greets them and...passes on." Again he waited for more, and then gathered the stones, repeating the process. As the stones settled he said, "Choose two stones and move them to wherever you are guided by your intuition."

Wode waited for Deera to make her selection and then studied the pebbles intently. "The sun is shining brightly... there are fish jumping in the lake...Another swan joins the first in flight and they swoop over her head…and land on the lake…The lake is now in an open plain…with big trees on the opposite bank, the steep sides of the valley have flattened out." There was silence for a while. "That's all I see. Does any of that make sense to you?"

"Yes it does." Her eyes were gleaming. "Thank you."

Wode got to his feet, brushing himself down. "Just clearing my energy." He put his hand on the colossal tree trunk for a minute or two, looking up at its vast girth receding into the sky before sitting back down opposite her again. He closed his eyes, let out a deep breath and went within; connecting to the Tree again.

Deera studied his strong face as he travelled the inner realm, and noticed a faint glow begin to surround him.

"Ask your question now." His voice was different – slow, low and deliberate.

"I feel a little embarrassed to ask now; I'm sure it's only trivial but it has been bothering me for months." Wode sat, saying nothing; eyes shut, a half-smile on his face.

"My question that I have been carrying is…How can I love more – I feel as though I have so much to give and nowhere to place my love."

Wode remained, eyes shut, a glowing statue waiting for the answer to come. The slow deep voice. "Your question, although simple, is one for us all, for all time. Thank you for being its questioner. It is a gift, for you were born in a year when the sun went out, in eclipse with the moon. You entered this realm on the day of the sixth full moon…at midnight…the feminine moon at her strongest and the father sun at his weakest…as timed by the ancient clock."

Deera took a deep breath and relaxed. She waited.

Wode continued, "Your love is within you, in its rightful place. You will never find love outside you. What you call 'your love' – that you think is personal to you – is a reflection of the Love of the Great Spirit, the Source, the One within you. Although what you think you love is outside you, it is just a reflection of your inner divine spirit – the You you are becoming. When you are loving, you are connecting to the universal Love, but you think it is just for a person or thing. That is the mind making the separation. For underneath the mind you are whole, One. Look into the space between your thoughts: there is your answer…"

Wode fell silent, waiting. All that could be heard were the sounds of nature: birds in the branches of the great Tree, bees hovering from flower to flower, sipping nectar from nature's sweet fountains, and the wind caressing the long, soft needles.

"You ask this question because you are more sensitive than most to the gift of bringing more love into this world. This is a question that no other could ask...As woman, your very nature is love, and yet you do not trust your real nature: you hold on to the past and that is all you see – you walk only looking at your feet. Lift your eyes in the present and see the landscape of love through which you walk; trust your feet will find the earth and you will be the love you seek. You have carried a glow over many lifetimes and softened the darkness in those around you. You show others the way with your light. You do not need to lead...you inspire...you shape...you guide as only the female can...The male can plan and stride off in his doing, but his way must be lit...You can light the way...but you need to let go of your past in this lifetime...It is burdening you, shrouding your spirit, your light...You feel thwarted by death but you will love again. It is your karma and gift to us all. Trust the wisdom of your spirit for it guides you from within."

Again Wode was silent for a time and then, "You journey well in this life...be calm of mind...connect with the oneness within you and you will be guided...Thank you for bearing the question and now the answer.... That is all."

Deera watched Wode with tears gently coursing down her face; the glow faded. He continued to sit there with eyes closed, his body gently swaying to an inner breeze. Eventually the moment began to fall away and he opened his eyes and leant forward to embrace her. It was a spontaneous gesture in recognition of a significant moment shared, and neither was keen to be the first to pull away.

In silence they made their way back towards her father. Harrell read the mood perfectly and said nothing as he came forward to embrace Wode farewell. Harrell had saddled the horses as he'd felt it appropriate to leave straight afterwards. Words spoken in divination dived deep into the pool of our Being and, the longer they remained undisturbed, the more they shaped our karma. Discussing the reading too soon could pull the imprint of the words from the depths and affect the flow of destiny.

"Thank you, Wode, for being here. I know you've changed her life. Thank you." Harrell reached forward and dropped a leather pouch into Wode's hand.

"I don't need payment," Wode said, and moved to return it.

Harrell held Wode's hands in his and looked him in the eye. "It isn't payment. It's a gift, and you might just need it."

Wode thanked him, slightly nonplussed, and said goodbye to Deera, who embraced him again before she mounted.

"Safe ride home."

"We're actually going to Tulkney first, to visit relatives," said Harrell.

"Then journey well," Wode said and beaming, he bowed low in a flamboyant gesture of courtesy. They waved, nudged their horses with their heels and took off at a steady trot, both the same and yet leaving different; a new destiny ahead.

Wistfully, Wode watched them go; he stood for a long time until they merged into the horizon. Gathering himself he looked down at the pouch in his hand and opened it to find gold coins. "Well, well, well. Thank you," Wode said out loud, and then turned his thoughts to Geeter, Berlen and Thrum.

## Chapter 7

*Vigilance is ultimately the only weapon.*

Wode only had to wait until the afternoon before the next Keeper of the Tree arrived. He was delighted. It was long enough for what he'd needed to do and short enough for him to get to Teksel as soon as he could. He'd seen a black kite circling in the sky above him all morning: Keekra. He sent her back to Geeter with the message that he was coming.

The new Keeper had arrived on horseback but left on foot. Wode had given a brief explanation for his need to hasten his return to Teksel and easily persuaded him to part with his mount for one of the gold coins from Harrell's pouch. Wode had thanked his new friend and, after allowing the horse a short feed and water, he adjusted the saddle and mounted.

"What's her name?"

"Tarn."

"Thank you again."

"It is my pleasure. Now be gone, my friend."

Wode needed no further bidding and urged Tarn on. She sensed his mood and went off at a steady canter. She kept it up all the way to the bottom of the escarpment on which Wode had stood looking down across the Tulrain, only three days before. From here he kept her at a fast walk until night camp.

He dismounted and removed her bridle. Loosening the saddle strap, he patted her neck and spoke to her. She lifted her head to listen.

"We're staying here the night; keep the fire in your sight at all times," and with that he let her loose and set about making a fire.

After some food, he went to work on Geeter, Berlen and Thrum. Only time would tell if he was successful.

---

The following night Wode was at the tavern in Teksel. It had been a hard ride and both he and Tarn were exhausted. She was stabled for the night with plenty of water and hay, and he was tucking into a good hot meal. He was just clearing his plate when a man came up and stood in front of him, casting a long shadow.

Wode lifted his head. "Moosen!"

"Hello, Wode, what brings you to these parts?"

Wode got up and embraced his friend. "Join me and I'll tell you. On your way to the Tree?"

Moosen nodded. "And you're just back?"

"Yes, I was only there two days for one questioner, which suited me fine. You look well."

Moosen sat down and Wode began to explain the situation, keeping his voice low. His friend sat glued to his every word and then all of a sudden sat bolt upright.

"This Rekle. Is she fair-haired, slightly haughty and with outspoken cheekbones?"

"Yes, do you know her?"

"From a long time ago. She was brought to me by her mother, who I sensed was keen for her to leave home. She had some ability and wanted me to assess her for apprenticeship. Her mother couldn't pay anything because she was very poor and so I agreed on the understanding that the girl would keep house too. I later found out that she'd been with old Donnat as well and that he'd been dismayed by her headstrong ways. He deemed her unsuitable for gnoseership and I was of the same opinion. I gave her a couple of months but she didn't have the temperament – too impatient and easily frustrated with the ancient ways we keep alive. I'm all for refining techniques but she was just in a hurry all the time and I was glad to be rid of her." He chuckled. "Who knows how many of us she spent time with, but enough to pick up some insight into sorcery for sure. And if someone is poisoning your man Berlen, I'd put my money on her."

"I cannot be sure yet. Berlen's wife died not long before it all started, so folk assume his strangeness is related to his sorrow. And it is true, he has sorrow in him but also a gratitude that she is out of pain, and a deeper knowledge of the reality of her passing over. He has also had the comfort of inner realm communication with her – their love keeps them enjoined." Wode pondered for a second. "No, I really do not believe his symptoms come from his mourning."

"I know there are few who can match you, Wode, but don't underestimate the Rekle woman. All that impatience in the first place and then failing gnoseership; she will have plenty of anger in her to direct your way."

"You are not wrong. Anyway…we shall see what we shall see." He looked at his companion. "Now what has kept Moosen busy?"

Moosen brought Wode up to date with his life and they talked long into the night before going their separate ways. Wode had always liked the older man; he was a good gnoseer and devoted to the people in his locale, and just before sleep overtook him he pondered Moosen's warning about Rekle the failed gnoseer.

Wode was up early when no one else was about in the tavern or the stable and he quietly led Tarn out onto the road. He made a brief stop at the bakery and then headed off into the country on the road beside the smithy. He kept her at a brisk walk for a short time before urging her into a canter. He was careful not to tire her out but keen to get to Geeter as soon as he could.

He arrived at Berlen's farm about an hour later and pulled up short of the brow of the final hill. Dismounting, he led Tarn into a copse beside a stream. He chose a tree that was far enough from others but close enough to the stream for her tether to reach it. She could eat, drink and not get the rope wound up around other trees. He took off the saddle and bag and placed them behind a bush.

"I am going to leave you here for a day or two – I am not sure how long exactly, but I will come as soon as I can. There are cows nearby, so you are not alone." She waggled her ears at him in response. "I know the cows aren't the same but I cannot go riding into the farm, it would not fit my story." He patted her on the rump, picked up his staff and pack, and left her already pulling contentedly at the grass. It was still early.

Wode stood at the top of the rise above the farm and surveyed the scene. He was just about to stride down the hill when he saw Rekle come out of the house and turn down a path beside a meadow. Something caught his attention above him. Kites! Geeter was following her. He watched. The birds stayed high, flying big circles above Rekle as she walked out of sight. She must have stopped, as they stayed circling in an ever tighter pattern. He marked the spot and waited until he caught sight of her returning to the farmhouse, and as soon as the door was closed he ran down the hill. He knocked loudly and walked right in, hoping to catch Rekle in the act of some evil-doing.

"Hello," he called out, making straight for the kitchen.

She was at the far end of the kitchen by some storage pots. "Ah Rekle," he said cheerfully. "I have fresh bread baked this morning, I left just after it came out of the oven." He could see she was flustered.

"Oh, hello, Orlech. You're back."

"Yes, we were working on a barn off the Kuik road. Nice fellow, that Turb." As fate would have it, Turb the carpenter was in the tavern last night and Wode had made a point of speaking to him.

"Yes he is. I believe he rebuilt the barns here a few years ago."

"So he was saying. How's Berlen?"

"He's not been good. I was about to take him up his medicine."

"Let me do that for you. I would like to see him." Wode left her no room to refuse.

"All right…here it is. Thank you."

"And is there anything else I can help you with today?"

"I'll think of something."

"Good, good," and Wode left the room.

He found Berlen sitting on the edge of his bed, head in hands, groaning.

"Hello, Berlen, it's Orlech."

"Who?"

"Orlech, Geeter's uncle."

"Oh yes. A bad head today," Berlen groaned. Wode sat down beside him, looking at him carefully; he wanted to convince the old man to stop taking the herbs. "How long have you been taking the medicine?"

"I don't remember, but it seems a long time."

"Does it seem to be helping?"

Berlen turned to look at Wode: the whites of his eyes had a yellowish hue. "Sometimes I think it does but overall..." He sighed. "I'm not so sure."

"Well, if it's not curing you, then it is not the right mixture and you might as well not be taking it."

"Mmm, you might be right."

"So I will throw this medicine away and we can tell Rekle, and see how you do. I will stay for a day or so if you like – to see you through."

"Thank you," Berlen said trustingly.

"Here's some water." Wode went to the jug beside the bed and poured out some water. As he did so he began to sing very quietly. He held the cup in both hands as he sang. Wode was using an ancient healing practice – emanating healing thoughts into the water. It was in-putting a healing vibration, to be held by the water in the cup and passed on to the water in the body of the one who was sick.

Berlen was a little bewildered but found the gentle song soothing, and he just sat there with head in hands, mesmerised by the song. Eventually Wode stopped singing and handed Berlen the cup.

"Drink it all down." Berlen did so.

"If you feel up to it, would you like me to accompany you on a short walk?"

"Yes, I could manage that. Thank you."

"I will just look in on Geeter and then bring you some breakfast."

"Thank you, Orlech. Good man."

Wode stepped quietly out and made his way to the room he and Geeter had shared.

He knocked. "Geeter, it's Orlech," he said, and entered.

Geeter was sitting on the bed with his eyes closed, still flying with Keekra, but he opened his eyes abruptly when Wode interrupted.

"Wo– Orlech!"

"Don't leave Keekra hanging."

"Oh. Right," and Geeter closed his eyes to thank her and say goodbye.

When he was done, Wode brought him up to date with

his news, skipping lightly over the events at the Wisdom Tree. "We will go out for a walk later with Berlen and see if we can find the plant that has been poisoning him so I can make up an antidote. We will depart tomorrow anyway and take him with us."

"To Tulkney?"

"No, we will have to go back to Athale."

Geeter sighed a sigh worthy of a seasoned actor. "I suppose my future will have to wait," he said, resigned.

———

They went down to share the bread with Rekle and afterwards Wode took Berlen some breakfast in his room.

"I feel a bit better, Orlech, and I've more appetite."

"That's good. Shall we go out after you have eaten?"

"Yes, let's do that," and Berlen started to eat.

"How do you feel about going to stay with Thrum and Keela for a while?"

"And leave the farm to Palt and Rekle? They'd ruin it."

"Have you really been able to keep an eye on things lately anyway?"

"Hmm. I don't mind not being able to help out. I've earned the rest. Not that fighting a sickness is much of a rest. I keep an eye on things from a distance – old Frillan, the cowherd, comes by every other day to give me a report when Palt's not around. Mind you, I have trouble remembering what he says with these headaches and the seeing things. Very confusing." Berlen finished his food in silence.

"Right, Berlen, let's go and on the way we will talk to Rekle."

"About what?"

"About you visiting your brother."

"Oh yes."

They went downstairs into the kitchen where Rekle was tidying up with Geeter's help.

Berlen took a deep breath. "Rekle, Orlech's offered to take me to Athale for a while – I could do with the change of scene. And I really can't take those herbs any more, they don't seem to be working. The herbalist must have it wrong."

Rekle turned to Wode, eyes blazing, "You are meddling in other people's business."

"I simply asked him if the herbs were doing any good and he said he didn't think so." Wode kept the truth short.

"Well, we'll see what Palt has to say about this," Rekle almost shrieked and stormed off.

"That was a bit excessive," Berlen observed, shaking his head. "Too headstrong for her own good."

Wode smiled to himself. "Shall we go for that walk?"

---

The day had been a strain for all concerned. Geeter was under the bedcovers and nearly asleep, and Wode was tired and lost in thought whilst getting ready for bed. He was reviewing the day: he had led the way along the path that he'd seen Rekle take earlier that morning. He'd marked the circling kites' position over the ground as being between two hawthorn trees, and sure enough, he'd found banewort. A leaf was enough to kill a man but it was bitter and only small amounts could be hidden in food without it being detected. Perhaps not enough to kill a man quickly…and as he looked closely, he'd been able to see where leaves had been torn from other plants in adjacent patches of banewort.

Whilst Berlen was out of earshot, Wode had asked, "Is this what you saw from above, Geeter?"

"Yes, two small trees…" Geeter had stopped to look from one to the other. "Yes, these are them. Rekle came here twice."

"Good lad, well done. Did you see Palt do anything strange?"

"No."

"I do not think Palt is aware of what his wife is doing," Wode had said. "She doesn't want to be a farmer's wife and she is obviously quite sure he doesn't want to be stuck in the country when he could be living the high life as a town merchant."

He'd gone on to tell Geeter about his meeting with Moosen, and how Rekle had tried and failed to become a gnoseer…

Sudden searing pain brought him back to the present. "Aaaahhh."

Geeter sat bolt upright, shocked out of near sleep. He saw Wode bent double sitting on the edge of his bed and watched in horror as his friend went grey, breaking out in a cold sweat. Right before his eyes he appeared to be transforming into a manic, wizened shell of a man. He started making frantic chopping motions with his hands around his waist, as if cutting invisible ropes attached to his body.

Geeter was in shock, his towering mentor crumbling and falling in agony before him. He sat helplessly, fighting off panic, and watched as Wode cried out again in tortured pain. The sound of Wode's agony sent shockwaves of alarm rippling through to his very being, shaking the hero within to rise, phoenix-like, out of the ashes of inaction.

"What can I do?" Geeter shouted, his words momentarily distracting Wode from his increasing agony.

"Got to get out of here," Wode panted, wincing. "Get all our things. Don't leave anything at all." He staggered to the door, grabbing his staff, and nearly fell through the door and down the stairs.

Geeter heard the front door open as he frantically packed up all Wode's belongings and stuffed his own things into his pack. He cast an eye around the room and, satisfied he had everything, grabbed the lantern, ran out of the room, down the stairs and out into the night.

He could hear Wode's faltering steps and groans up the road to his left. He ran fast to catch up. Wode was staggering several steps and then stopping to battle spasms of pain. He was retching and coughing and panting, staggering from one fall to the next. It seemed to take ages but Wode found what he was looking for and stumbled off the road to his left. He found the stream and collapsed close by.

"Pack," Wode panted. Geeter quickly placed it beside him.

Wode looked up, inclining his head to the left. "Over there is a horse. To the left a bush…behind it a saddlebag, and make a fire. Quick, can't hold out much longer."

Geeter worked fast to scrape some leaves and twigs together, he took the candle from the lantern and lit the leaves, piling on the twigs and nearly smothering the burgeoning flames in his haste. Satisfied that the fire was going, he darted to retrieve the saddlebag and knelt down beside Wode, who now had his eyes closed.

"Wode!" He shook the gnoseer vigorously. Wode opened his eyes and slowly reached out for the saddlebag. Geeter took charge and opened it and drew out a bundle. He looked questioningly at Wode, who nodded.

Geeter opened the bundle to reveal an assortment of stones of varying sizes, none bigger than an egg, and Wode reached forward, crying out again in pain, to select a pure white quartz, the size of a plum.

Wode grabbed his knife and thrust it into the fire. Geeter watched in horror as Wode, eyes bulging, started shouting; angrily, unintelligibly and upsetting Tarn, who whinnied and backed away to the end of her tether. Suddenly the shouting stopped and after a heartbeat of complete silence, Wode began to writhe as if wrestling an invisible opponent on whom he was unable to get a hold; and then equally suddenly, he was still. Momentarily, he looked at Geeter almost normally through the madness he was battling, and Geeter detected Wode's willpower sustaining him, driving him on: the patient was also the healer.

"Water." Geeter searched for his flask and handed it to Wode, who took a long draught, coughing up half of it before leaning forward to remove the knife from the fire.

Geeter watched transfixed as Wode poured water on the knife until it stopped sizzling and steaming, and then pulled his shirt up and aside to reveal his belly. Wode again writhed with inner demons before settling again to bring the knife towards his navel.

Geeter panicked. There was an urge in him to dive across the space between them and wrestle the knife out of Wode's shaking hand, but something kept him back, and all he could do was look on as Wode made the cut. Dark blood oozed out of the inch-long incision before Wode placed the white quartz stone over it, holding it in place.

Geeter, looking on, sensed a change in Wode who began to quietly weep, and then sob – the abyss of grief for Mara and his son released in tears coursing down his cheeks. In time the tears slowed and he began filling his lungs with deep breaths of sweet night air. And then suddenly he would turn again – shouting and ranting, shaking with the force of anger and rage coming into him. But still Wode held the stone in place.

As his shock began to wear off, Geeter too started to weep, releasing the trauma of what he was witnessing: the fright of it all, his hero and mentor and second chance of a father declining into a ranting ape of raw black festering emotion. Now and then he got up to gather some more sticks to put on the fire, but otherwise he just sat and hoped for his friend to return.

As the night wore on, Wode became quieter and quieter – a comparative peace varying only with him panting periodically like a distressed dog gulping in lungfuls of air. His eyes remained closed, but now and then he would look down and peel the stone away from the wound to check the bleeding. And then eventually there was silence.

As the dawn began to promise, Wode fell asleep for a time and then awoke to examine the wound. Satisfied, he put his knife into the embers of the fire and dug around, coming away with a small lump of hot grey ash balanced on the blade. Carefully, he pulled the wound together and, dropping the ash onto the clotting wound, placed a bigger stone over it. He winced with the pain but leant over to rummage in his pack for a long piece of cloth, which he used to bandage himself.

"Geeter!" The boy sat up quickly, shaking the sleep from his head. "I need more water."

Geeter picked up the empty flask and went to the nearby stream to refill it. He brought it back to Wode and knelt down beside him. Wode drank thirstily and smiled weakly but reassuringly at his concerned young friend.

Relieved to see him smile, Geeter couldn't contain his need to know. "What happened, Wode?"

"Sorcery! A black-art dart from Rekle."

Geeter looked puzzled. "What's that?"

From the pit of exhaustion, Wode slowly and haltingly explained, for he knew learning in the moment was the perfect time for Geeter to acquire this knowledge – it may never come around again. "With the intent of evil… someone practised in the art of working with energy… can fire a dart with the purpose of harming another…Evil exists because it has a force sustaining it…and that force can be directed at someone, if you know how…That's why before I sleep, I always pull down my shieldagh… Rekle got me before I'd done it." He paused to rest and breathe deeply; his energy was fading fast.

"An evil dart can create a bridge…connecting the victim into the part of the inner realm…where black, old emotional pain resides – festering aeons of negative emotion…left behind by people on their death…and it travels across the bridge into the victim…and unchecked it moves into their body, sucking the life out of them for its own gain…. That's why you saw me trying to chop the connecting ties with my hands…It is the most terrifying feeling and I remember it from my training with Worian."

"Do you know how to do it?"

Wode nodded. "Yes, all gnoseers do, it's part of our long training, but we never use dark energy. We know the consequences." He paused, exhausted. "Listen out for a cart later this morning and stop it when it comes," and with that his eyes closed and he slumped back, spent.

Geeter sat dazed and bewildered, running through the night's events — safely cocooned in the warm glow of relief at the amazing transformation of his friend, who had come back from the precipice of hell. Images of hundreds of re-forming bridges of evil emotion played on his mind and he shuddered at what he saw, feeling the clawing temptation to engage with this mesmerising shadow. Shaking himself out of its treacly grip, he too lay down and fell into a deep enveloping sleep.

## Chapter 8

*Karma — our returning friend.*

∽∽

Geeter awoke with a start to the sound of Tarn urinating. He looked round to see the horse eyeing him quietly. They stared at each other as Geeter's disorientated mind tried to work out where he was, and then it all came flooding back. He got up to check on Wode, who was as still as a corpse but still warm with life. Relieved, Geeter began reviving the fire which had burnt down to a few glowing embers when he heard the sound of a cart approaching. He ran into the road to see a large farm cart coming steadily up the hill leading a tethered horse. There were two men in the seat, the bigger man holding the reins.

"Geeter!"

He squinted into the light, trying to recognise the driver.

"Geeter, it's Thrum."

"THRUM!" Geeter was overjoyed with surprise and relief. He recognised Chet too. "You've come!"

"Yes, lad, we've come," said Thrum as they jumped down. Geeter rushed up to him and threw his arms around his chest.

"It's all right, lad, we're here to help," said a bemused Thrum, raising an eyebrow at Chet. "Where's Wode?"

"Thank God you've come, we think we've saved Berlen but Wode nearly died last night." It all came out in a bit of a rush, the words tumbling out in the right order by a miracle.

"Nearly died? Wode?" Thrum was shocked. He gripped Geeter by the shoulders. "What happened? Where is he?"

"Here," and Geeter ran off the road into the small clearing, with Thrum and Chet close behind, to where Wode was still lying under his blanket.

Thrum and Chet took in the scene: Wode's pack contents strewn beside him, a white bloodied stone, Wode's knife close by and blood on Wode's hands. Thrum knelt down beside his supine friend. He was worried it might be too late. He put his ear beside Wode's mouth to check his breathing.

"He's fast asleep," Thrum whispered. He got up, reassured. "Chet, lead the horses off the road. We'll have some breakfast and Geeter can tell us what has been going on."

"How did you know to come?"

"Well I reckon Wode here did that dream message thing a couple of nights ago, because I saw him in my sleep calling my name and sitting beside a sick Berlen. He just kept calling me over and over again to come to Berlen. So here I am!"

"Thank God you did. It's been a horrific night," and Geeter related all that had happened since coming to Berlen's farm; that Wode had suspected Rekle was poisoning Berlen with banewort, and they'd found the banewort plants with leaves torn off.

"So what happened last night?"

"It was really strange. One minute I'm just about to fall asleep and Wode is sitting on his bed and the next minute he's doubled up in pain from a black-art dart. I think Rekle fired something into him when his guard was down…"

"Rekle?!"

"Yes, Wode found out that she's a failed gnoseer, and we just got out of the house as quickly as we could and Wode staggered up here where he'd left his pack. He then started performing some sort of miracle remedy to save himself. Which is what the blood and stones are all about," Geeter added, shivering at the memory. "It was horrible – he was shouting, ranting and sobbing until he finally fell asleep around dawn. But I reckon he saved himself from whatever it was."

"Water!"

They all turned round in surprise and knelt beside the pale and drawn gnoseer. Geeter handed a flask to Wode, who took a long draught and then lay back. He looked up at them with an exhausted smile. "Is there any breakfast left?"

"Aye, Wode there is," said Thrum. "We have bread and eggs aplenty. Chet, set to."

Soon Wode was eating and the colour returned to his face. "You made good time, Thrum."

"Well, I was left in no doubt as to the urgency of the situation and, when I awoke after that dream, I just told Keela that I needed to rescue Berlen. We had a little discussion, packed some provisions, talked to Chet who volunteered to come and harnessed up my fastest horses. For an ageing farmer, I can move quickly when I need to," he chuckled.

They all finished eating and began to pack up. Wode gingerly got up and washed his medicine stones in the stream before carefully returning them to his medicine bundle.

"What will happen to Berlen now?" Geeter asked.

"You'll find out. Come on, we'd better get to the house before she finishes him off."

As Chet and Thrum manoeuvred the cart and horses back onto the road, Geeter gathered their belongings together and untethered Tarn. Leaning heavily on his staff, Wode followed slowly to the road and carefully clambered onto the back of the cart. With legs dangling, Geeter and Wode rode side by side the short distance to the farmhouse, with Tarn trotting along behind.

Thrum pulled up outside the front of the house and handed the reins to Chet before jumping down and striding purposefully up to the open front door. He hesitated a second before marching straight into the hallway.

"Berlen, dear brother, it's Thrum." And he went straight up the stairs to Berlen's room.

Rekle was in the kitchen and looked surprised and annoyed at this early unwelcome intrusion as Chet and Geeter walked in. But her face turned suddenly pale in genuine shock on seeing Wode following on behind. She looked like a trapped animal unable to escape – she knew the power of a black-art dart.

"I notice your utter surprise to see me, Rekle." Wode paused. "Well, if there was any doubt, your face is confirmation enough that you fired the black dart into me." He was speaking quietly but the power and intensity of his voice would have carried a field away.

Thrum came into the kitchen. "Berlen's just coming. Where's Palt?" He ignored Rekle.

There were hurried footsteps in the hallway and Palt strode into the kitchen, a puzzled frown on his face.

"Hello, uncle, I heard voices. What on earth is going on?"

"I'll save my explanations until your father is here." Thrum looked at him sternly, his voice as hard as granite. "Sit down, everyone." At which point Berlen came in and was helped to his chair. Thrum remained standing; he had the air of a warrior king, and everyone's attention.

"Well, Palt, what is going on is that someone has been poisoning your father." His nephew's jaw dropped and his mouth moved but no words came out. He was the only one in the room genuinely shocked.

"W–what do you mean? Why?" Palt stared at Thrum and then at Rekle, who was unable to look him in the eye.

"Your wife here has been quietly poisoning your father, so that you can get your hands on the farm without having to wait for his natural death."

Now Berlen looked shocked. Rekle broke the stunned silence.

"It's a lie, Palt! A lie. I'd never do such a thing to your father."

Palt's mind was a whirlwind of confusion.

Wode got to his feet. They all watched as he walked slowly across the room. He stopped in front of some storage jars and then slowly reached behind one to pull out a gathering cloth. He walked back to the kitchen table and began to unravel the folds of the cloth, opening it out to reveal one partially dried leaf and several leaf fragments.

"This is your gathering cloth, Rekle. Perhaps you'd like to sample some of this leaf?" He picked it up and brought it over to her.

"That's not my cloth. I don't have one. It must be yours, you knew where it was." Rekle turned to implore the others. "I've never seen it before."

Wode held it closer and Rekle just stared back at him, defiant yet afraid. She stood her ground as he brought it closer still. "Why won't you try some? Is it because you know what it is?"

"I don't know what you are talking about."

"Yes you do, it's banewort and I've seen you picking it," shouted Geeter.

Wode brought it ever closer to her face. "It is banewort, isn't it, Rekle?" Her eyes widened with fear and she eventually turned her head away.

"If taken in small quantities it produces confusion, poor balance, headaches, delirium, hallucinations and so on. All these Berlen has experienced over the past few months. A small enough dose to make him ill but not enough to kill him," Wode explained.

Rekle was desperate. She'd never felt so estranged from all she knew. Never so alone. "I didn't meant to kill him, just to make him ill enough to leave."

"God!" exclaimed Thrum with fists clenched, just managing to restrain himself from lunging at her. "Well, you two are the ones leaving now."

"I don't believe it," said Palt. "You would make my father ill on purpose?"

Like a cornered animal with nothing to lose, Rekle lashed out, her face hardening as the venom spilled out of her. "Well you were the one going on about how you preferred town life and that you'd sell the farm and use the money to start trading in Kuik. I just wanted to bring that day forward for you. And you have been planning it since seeing him ill, haven't you?"

Palt, wide-eyed, was horrified at the change in her, but he knew that what she said was true: he had planned to sell the farm. Without a word, looking stunned and pale, Palt got to his feet and left the room.

Rekle stared at Palt's departing back and then looked defiantly around the room before hurrying out.

The silence hung in the air, filling the room with a deafening nothing. Thrum took a deep breath and blew out of the side of his mouth. He put a big rough hand on his brother's shoulder. "Berl, you can either come home with me, or if you'd prefer, Chet's willing to stay and help you get back on your feet."

"Thank you, brother, that's kind of you." Berlen considered a moment. "I don't feel like going anywhere just yet." He turned to his nephew. "Chet, I'd appreciate a hand if you'd stay a few weeks."

Chet nodded. "I'd be glad to, Uncle Berl."

———

Over the next few days Berlen grew in strength. The poison was slowly leaving his system, his mind no longer preoccupied with his own death, leaving his body free to recover. Thrum had taken Tarn and rode with Palt and Rekle as far as Teksel and made enquiries about the housekeeper who had helped out after Fabrayer's death. She was horrified to hear of Berlen's poisoning but delighted to be the first to spread the news around Teksel. As it happened, she was able to return to Berlen's farm immediately, not having found work elsewhere, and she soon had the house looking like a proper home again.

Wode rested for the next two days, venturing out for short walks and being careful not to tire himself. He had drawn on an almighty well of strength to perform the remedy to Rekle's sorcery. Dark energy could penetrate every cell, and to clear it from the body required powerful resources. Only Geeter, who had witnessed the events of that night, understood the depth of Wode's fatigue and left him alone to recuperate.

Geeter spent time with Chet, learning about farming, and in return showing him his gift with birds, and even introducing him to Keekra. At the evening meal on the second day Chet told his father, "You've got to see Geeter and his birds. He called a black kite out of the sky and it landed on his arm!"

"Where d'you learn that, Geeter?"

"Wode showed me."

"Proper little gnoseer, aren't you? What says you, Wode?" Geeter glowed.

"Indeed, the birds are drawn to him and he learns well."

"Well, Geeter, to learn you have to have the desire, and if you have the desire you can do anything your karma allows. Eh, Wode?"

"It is true that, as we live our life, the karmic load changes and this does suggest that anything is possible. In fact, if you remove all traces of doubt – all traces – you can accomplish incredible things."

Geeter's eyes were sparkling. "Can you train me to be a gnoseer, Wode?"

"We will see what your mother says." Wode saw the sparkle fade a little and he endeavoured to reassure him. "Remember Mairhi's words, Geeter, 'Spirit knows what you need'. Nothing that wasn't meant for you will pass you by."

Geeter's mother held the key of destiny to his unfolding path and he was afraid she'd lock the door on his new dreams for ever, and throw away the key.

―――――

Before he and Geeter left, Wode performed an energy clearance on the house – cleansing it of the heavy negative energy he'd noticed when they arrived. He had Geeter join him as he walked around the house burning sage, using an eagle feather to waft the cleansing smoke into nooks and crannies where unwanted influences could lurk. Explaining what he was doing, he opened all the doors and windows and walked from room to room, looking through narrowed eyes and singing quietly under his breath. If he saw a shadow of negative energy, he pulled down a ball of light from above his head and hurled it with breath and arm at the offending darkness; the light encircled the shadow and dissolved it.

Geeter was not able to see the dark energy that Wode was clearing but he was fascinated and in awe of the explanation. "It's a similar technique that I perform on people with negative shadows in their aura which are causing them distress."

"Why didn't you simply do this on Rekle?"

"That's a good question. Well, in all animals, including humans, it requires their permission to perform such a remedy, otherwise it simply does not work. It is their karma to have that negative energy to take them down a path of learning, and as long as they 'want' it, it is theirs.

To change it against their will is to play with the balance of a life – something not to be entered into lightly, as the responsibility for that portion of karma can fall to you. The way I see it – there is my business, other people's business and Spirit's business, and until invited otherwise that is really the best way to keep it."

Geeter listened intently, soaking every drop from the experience, and once the house was devoid of any negative influences, Wode set about clearing Berlen's system of poison.

"Berlen, your body will right itself in the next few weeks as it regenerates from the poison's damage. I will clean your energy field to make it happen more quickly and effectively. Also, I have made up a herbal remedy for you in the kitchen. Just dilute a spoonful with water twice a day until it is gone."

"Thank you, Wode," Berlen said gratefully. He was sitting on the side of his bed, relieved at the change in his health and looking forward to the future, something he'd not been able to do since the death of Fabrayer. "Thank you."

Wode smiled at him. "I'm glad you are feeling better," and he gestured for Berlen to lie down. Once settled, Wode covered him in a blanket, pulled down his shieldagh over him and went to work. Berlen watched briefly as the gnoseer began to slowly move his hands a few inches above his body before closing his eyes. Wode was looking off into the distance, seeing an inner picture as he scanned the old man's energy through his hands; his inner senses were reaching way beyond the ability to feel warmth and cold, or the movement of breeze over skin. He felt for energy holes which he patched with energy from his shieldagh, and blocked energy gates down the centre of the body, which he cleaned out and restored. Wode had only been working a couple of minutes when he noticed Berlen's breathing change. As he slipped blissfully into a deep sleep, Wode knew before long he'd be dreaming with Fabrayer.

---

"Thank you, Wode," said Thrum.

"And thank you," Wode responded. They clasped each other by the hand and shoulder. It was time to part again. Geeter and Wode said their goodbyes and mounted.

Berlen had given Geeter a horse called Eska, as thanks for his part in his deliverance, and to Wode he'd promised some golden chilluns if he ever got married again. "You never know what life has coming, Wode," he chuckled.

"And Fabrayer insisted – she spoke to me in a dream!"

"Thank you, Berlen." Wode adjusted himself gingerly in the saddle – he was still a long way from full strength. "Please thank Keela for the extra food, Thrum."

"Aye, I will. Farewell."

"Goodbye, Chet, look after your uncle."

"Surely. Ride well," and with that they turned the horses towards Tulkney for Geeter's journey home.

## Chapter 9

*Not all time follows the flight of an arrow.*

❧

Teksel was several hours behind them. Their pace was easy as they rode west, enjoying each other's company after the drama at Berlen's farm; the energy of their shared experience invoking a perpetually renewing rapport, sealing an unseen bond of camaraderie that began to blur the line of teacher and pupil. Sitting in Thrum and Keela's kitchen discussing Geeter's future seemed a long time ago. They were back to the original plan – to return Geeter to his mother. Geeter wanted to hurry. He had missed her greatly despite the strong will of destiny pulling him away, and he wanted her blessing to apprentice Wode as a future gnoseer.

"What will happen to Rekle?"

"Well, she will probably convince Palt that she was not actually trying to kill his father. She could have done it quite easily at any time. She will have set up a karma that won't be favourable: Palt might be too wary of her and they might part; she might attract a terrible illness, an accident…it is up to the great karmic wave of life. What you put in your well is what you must drink."

Geeter looked at Wode in doubt; a big question had just occurred to him and he wasn't sure if…

"Ask it, Geeter."

Geeter nearly jumped out of his skin; he still wasn't used to having his thoughts so easily read. "I was just thinking, have you asked yourself why it was that Mara died?"

"Yes."

Geeter summoned his courage. "Er…and…did you come to a reason?"

Wode shifted in his saddle. "Often a cherished soul agrees to take on a role in the next life for us, to play a part in order to set up circumstances that will benefit our learning. The details are so finely tuned that both souls and others benefit from the roles played. So the soul in Mara and mine as me agreed in another place to meet and be in love and live together for the time we did, for our mutual soul growth."

Geeter was quiet for a while. Wode knew what was coming next and brought Tarn to a standstill. "So my father, for some reason, agreed to die to benefit me or my mother in some way."

Wode reached out and put a hand gently on his shoulder. "It is possible, yes." He smiled at him. "You see, it is the challenges in life that shape us; without hardship we would not realise our inner strengths; without the roughness of stone our blade is not sharpened. Reflect on what you have learnt since you left home: self-reliance, determination, courage...and of course your gift with birds. You want to be a gnoseer?"

"Yes, more than anything."

"Well if your father had not died, you would still be on your old farm and we would not have met. Your father was like a tree for your destiny and you must now take that tree and carve yourself a boat on which to float on the sea of life. You must make oars and a mast – for Life will provide the wind to carry you on."

"I had better be a gnoseer then, hadn't I?" Geeter announced, like a newly crowned boy king.

"Well your beloved father's passing might have been for another reason beyond our knowledge. Nothing is certain," counselled his chief adviser.

"It all seems very complicated." Geeter's puffed-up self deflating with a sigh.

"Geeter, you are still young and with a universe of knowledge to discover. There are few adults who really know karma, let alone youngsters your age."

Geeter received the backhanded compliment and smiled gratefully up at Wode.

"Thanks, Wodey!"

"You cheeky little—" and with that Wode whacked Eska on the rump and the horse shot off with Geeter bouncing in the saddle, his laughter fading into the distance.

Wode smiled and shook his head at his growing affection for the lad. "Well, Life, this was unexpected." He'd not anticipated a fondness for someone developing so soon, let alone for a runaway boy. He looked to the heavens. "Is this my substitute for a son?" he wondered. How his life had changed, and in such a short time. Ah the magic of the solrom, he thought ruefully. He'd heard many a minstrel's song heralding the solrom travels of men through the ages – the emotional anguish, the extraordinary exploits and adventures, the distant lands seen, the romances, and the new ideas they returned with; if they did return. He had simply started to walk one day, wanting to be alone, to get away, to begin again…

Wode called a halt two hours before sunset. He was still below full strength after the black-art dart and needed more rest than normal. In fact both were secretly quite pleased for the excuse, as their buttocks were unused to the long saddle time. Wode's had suffered on his return journey from the Wisdom Tree and this was just compounding it. Maybe we will walk a bit tomorrow, thought Wode, as his legs and buttocks groaned with the initial stiffness after dismounting.

They found a beautiful glade off the road about fifty paces through some bushes, lined with pine and birch and the occasional oak. Tethering and unsaddling the horses, they set about making a camp for the night, gathering wood and starting a fire. Later, after food, a big bright waning moon rose languidly above the trees.

"When I was young I was fascinated by the fact the moon changed shape and got smaller and smaller, and then disappeared altogether. And then to return, getting fuller and fuller. In Brennan, the moon disappears behind the highland mountains and my father told me there were carpenters up there shaving the moon's shape smaller and smaller. And that the white moon dust fell on the mountains as it passed. He said the moon was a living thing and grew back time after time since forever."

Somehow thinking he would get a better view, Geeter got to his feet and stood gazing up for several minutes. "I can't see them, Wode, they must be very small." He continued to stand, full of contentment, looking up with a big smile on his face.

When a minute or two had passed, Wode finally asked, "What are you doing?"

"Emanating. I'm smiling the moon."

Wode chuckled to himself. "Good thing, Geeter. Well keep it up, I'm going to sleep."

They awoke early the following morning and started out at a leisurely pace, energy renewed. Clouds were building over the highlands and the temperature was dropping but rain was a day or two away yet.

As Tarn walked, the rhythm of her gently swaying body had Wode humming and he soon broke into song. He sang of times gone by and ancient answers to nature's mysteries. Geeter listened, lulled by the gentleness and tone of Wode's voice.

"Do you know 'How To Move A Mountain'?" asked Wode. Geeter shook his head.

Wode cleared his throat and began. The song's simple, captivating melody held Geeter's attention and he sat contentedly by as his gnoseer friend's voice floated on the air around them like fresh pollen seeking a home.

> *How to move a mountain?*
> *Is it beyond the will of man?*
> *A'first you look beyond your mind*
> *To a time the ancients can,*
> *To a time the ancients can.*
>
> *She's shroud' in snow, and rain*
> *Does fall, the streams run fast and long.*

*They carve her waist and sides and all,*
*As the centuries carry her song,*
*The centuries carry her song.*

*Rivulets carry her grain by grain*
*As she gives to the valley below.*
*Sweet Mother, dear giver of life to us all*
*'Queaths her flesh to the lands below,*
*Her flesh to the lands below.*

*The years do tumble about her head,*
*Outliving any man or beast.*
*So no one sees her stately walk*
*Through forests and valleys to the sea,*
*Through forests and valleys to the sea.*

*But if you go within so deep,*
*To where the ancients call,*
*You'll see her stately walk o'er time*
*As she nourishes beasts and all,*
*As she nourishes beasts and all.*

As the last notes drifted off into the distance, they continued on in silence, minutes growing unnoticed into the infinite passing of time.

The wide landscape was home to distant hamlets, fields and pastures that kept woods and wild ground apart like slow-moving wrestlers; it was easy-going for the horses and they made good progress. Alternating between riding and walking, they encountered few folk along the way and even fewer words passed between them. As the sun neared its zenith, they halted to take food and water, and afterwards stretched out to rest.

"How far to the Tulrain?" Geeter was feeling the plague of restlessness.

"We will probably be taking lunch on the riverbank, don't you worry."

"And then is it another day or so beyond to Tulkney?"

"Yes, about that, and…" Suddenly Wode was quiet. He went very still and Geeter immediately realised something wasn't right. Like a lone wolf sensing danger, Wode slowly got to his feet, his every sense reaching out to its fullest. He gestured palm down for Geeter to lie still as he uncoiled his body to full height.

"Your senses are good, my friend." A stranger's voice, tense and a way off.

"Maybe," Wode shouted back, scanning the woods and

rocks. "What do you want?" The seconds ticked by.

"I mean you no harm."

"Then why is an arrow to your bow?"

"Well, you can't be too careful in these parts…I see two horses, tell your companion to stand."

Wode gestured for Geeter to comply and lowered his voice. "Lone bowman…Keep your distance from me; it is harder to find you as a target if he starts shooting."

"Move into the road."

"I will…He is only a boy."

"Just keep where I can see you then, boy, and no one will get hurt. Both of you start walking backwards away from the horses."

"Not until you show yourself." Wode had picked him out even though he was well concealed, but he needed a better view. He sensed the man was alone, frightened and desperate; a dangerous combination. Wode watched as the man slowly, warily, moved out into the middle of the road, and Wode did the same. Fifty yards of clear road separated them.

"Now walk backwards away from the horses."

"Geeter, move back five paces and then stop." Wode didn't move.

As Geeter walked slowly backwards, he couldn't help but notice the air around him appearing to become warmer and that there was a slight glow around Wode.

"You aren't moving." The man sounded angry. "Move. Now."

"What do you want?"

"What you have."

"And what is that?"

"Nobody travels without means. Now start walking or I'll shoot."

Wode remained unmoved, a statue of complete vigilance, the glow around him becoming more visible. "Shoot away. I have nothing of any value to you. You can tell by our clothes we are not from wealth."

"If you don't back away, I'll shoot and split your heart in two."

"That is dangerous talk, friend; can I suggest you lower your bow and withdraw."

"I'm a good shot, I warn you, and I have your heart in my sights."

"I don't believe you are that accurate; you don't have the temperament."

"Try me."

Geeter was wondering why Wode just didn't do as the man said. He didn't want to see his friend killed, to be alone again. Yet he was mesmerised by the deadlock and the barely perceptible light beside Wode, who was now very slowly bending his arms upwards at the elbow.

"If you shoot that arrow, you will see more of me than you bargained for."

Silence. Time slowed, nature poised. The silence when time stands still is the silence of eternity; nothing exists in the eternity of now except the possibility of all things.

Geeter was staring at the man, his heart pounding in his ribcage like a madman trying to escape a closed room. Suddenly he saw the bowman's fingers straighten, releasing the string. The bow immediately sprang back into shape, sending its deadly missile hurtling towards Wode. Geeter was transfixed: instantly everything seemed more alive, the colours – the green of the leaves, the blueness of the sky – richer; the sunlight more golden, the air even clearer. Time slowed as the arrow flew...

Geeter's attention focused on the arrow's flight. Out of the corner of his eye, he was aware of Wode moving in slow motion. He was leaning to his right whilst his upper body twisted left, his arms windmilling up and over in one fluid motion to snatch the arrow out of the air inches from his chest.

Wode immediately broke into a run with two identical figures running either side of him, matching him stride for stride. He seemed to move at enormous speed towards the archer who was stuck in the immovable stillness of shock: the certainty of his arrow hitting its target completely and utterly destroyed. As Wode hunted down the ground between them, the archer's mind was frantically trying to catch up: aware of the figures coming towards him yet still not able to move until suddenly, a split second later, he caught up with reality and his body moved like a startled animal into the totality of running; legs fuelled by the terror of being pursued by an arrow-catching demon with two identical accomplices. He was running on pure instinct and left the road seeking the safety of bushes and trees as fast as his legs could carry him.

Wode reached the spot where his attacker disappeared into the bushes and stopped, immediately becoming "one" again. He stood listening to the man crashing through the undergrowth until he heard no more and, satisfied he would not return, began retracing his steps. He was panting hard and clutching his belly as Geeter ran up to him, a concerned look on his face.

"Are you hurt?"

"No, it's nothing, only that dart wound again." Wode put a reassuring hand on the boy's shoulder. "It is just not completely right yet and I have not had to move that quickly for a long time."

"You run fast and…how did you do that?" Geeter mimicked Wode snatching the arrow out of the air, as if he were swatting a fly.

Wode, still panting, grinned down at him. "Well he told me what he was aiming for, my heart, and that always helps but…" He looked over his shoulder. "Although I don't expect we shall see him again, just in case, we will ride on a bit and I will tell you the rest later. It is a nice trick, isn't it?"

"NICE? It's amazing!"

Eagerly Geeter hurried to pack up and was the first to remount. They proceeded at a good trot for a mile or so before slowing the horses to a walk. Continuing in silence for a while, Wode was fully aware that Geeter was bursting with curiosity beside him; a thirst for the knowledge of what he had just witnessed.

Finally, unable to contain his curiosity any longer, Geeter asked, "Can you tell me now?"

Wode smiled across at his young friend. "Very well, but first tell me, what did you see?"

"I saw you turn the tables on a man who was about to rob us by catching an arrow. I saw you then run after him, with what looked like two other Wodes, frightening the life out of him." Geeter paused. "And although part of me was in disbelief, I also seemed to be more aware, more alive than ever; the sky, the trees, everything seemed more…" He searched for a word. "Er…more alive, more vivid. And I had a sense that somehow all of it was possible for me and that you would teach me how to do it." He looked across at Wode triumphantly at the last part.

Wode chuckled at the boy's increasing confidence. "You see well, Geeter. And I may teach you yet, but the most important thing is that you were still conscious of being vividly conscious. That cannot really be taught, but it is something that all can learn by paying attention to the moving parts."

"What do you mean?"

"When you whittle a stick, for instance, if you do not have all your attention on the point at which your knife is in contact with the wood, you are not in the present. You are off thinking about something. And if you are not present, you are not really there, and if you aren't there, you cannot create – you won't be allowing the pure flow of creative energy, that pure flow of genius, into you, to produce something of form and beauty. You will cut too much off, or your finger, and curse your luck and not see it as your lack of presence at fault. Creativity is a gift, it is given – it is not us doing it – it happens through us."

He looked at his young protégé. "When I was standing there facing the man with his bow drawn, I was in the timeless present."

"I don't understand."

"Being totally present is a place deep inside us where time slows completely – a realm where we are totally in our senses, where we are not relying on our mind's interpretation of what the senses – sight, hearing, taste – are telling us: no thought, pure instinct. It is the mind's interpretation, although fast, that creates time. The present is the place of instinctive intelligence, and in that 'place' I had caught the arrow at the same time as it left the bow. The apparent time elapsed was created by your brain."

Wode saw a slightly blank look on Geeter's face. "Don't think about it, Geeter, just take the idea and you will find the knowledge will be revealed to you later. For like us all, you are born with a greater wisdom than you can ever know, and you have access to it at any time. You just have to find the path."

Wode halted Tarn, swung his leg over and slid down to the ground. He gestured for Geeter to join him and they tied the horses to a bush.

"Now, let me see if I can explain it to you in a different way." He was looking around for a stick. He selected one and drew a circle on the ground with lines cutting across the middle to reveal the circle's centre.

"See this as a wheel and these as the spokes that support the wheel's rim. The outer rim, the metal band, is your outer awareness into the world through the senses – sight, sound, smell…and just inside the rim is the beginning of your inner realm – where you think and dream, and where the emotions are. If you travel down a spoke – inside of yourself – to the centre, you will notice that thoughts pass more slowly, become less frequent and eventually disappear. This is where we go in deep dreamless sleep and if you go inside like this consciously, like in proper meditation, you reach a place that is still, no movement."

"Like a carriage wheel, with the spokes moving forward yet the wheel's centre appears still?"

"Exactly. As you move further back along the spoke to the rim, you come more and more into time. Be the centre and everything is still, and there is all the time necessary to act."

"Mmm." Geeter looked pensive. "I see what you mean."

"Good. That is all you need for now."

"And what about the other Wodes that appeared beside you?"

Wode smiled. "Pure magic. Well there is a place in Spirit – that place of pure stillness deep inside you, near the centre of the wheel," he said, pointing to the origin of the circle on the ground, "where your soul – the light that you are – can be realised. It is a place of pure wonder beyond the limits of normal mind and imagination. It is a place we withdraw into when our body dies, and it is a place gnoseers can access immediately. We help others be there too by guiding slowly and gently down the inner realm. It is here that you can relearn what you intended to learn in this lifetime, see lessons learnt from past lifetimes and connect with souls that you love. Because it is a place of pure love, free of dimensions like time and movement.

"It is here that we plan the lessons we wish to learn, what karma we wish to take on in order for us to progress. You see, we not only progress through one lifetime, we progress in soul consciousness: the more times our soul, the light that we are, recurs in a body to live through a life, the bigger the light becomes and the more powerful and deeper, or denser, the colour becomes. Now, when we are born into a body, we have divided our light: usually most of it is in the soul in the body living the life, and a smaller part remains in spirit – the place of lights – and we are connected to this part by a thread of invisible light. When we die, the soul that we are withdraws from the body along the light thread, to be made whole again with our part left in spirit. Old souls have the power and capacity to divide their light into more than one light body at once; or that light in spirit can be divided temporarily to produce copies in the world. That's what you saw me do."

"Incredible!"

"Indeed. It is a 'trick' most gnoseers can perform and often a necessary one to escape such situations."

"So do gnoseers carry any weapons to protect themselves?"

"By and large, no. We rely on our speed of intelligence – the ability to travel down the spokes of the wheel – to change the situation in our favour. We know the power and legacy of karma and, if we take a life in defending our own, we know that killing has to be paid for. Only the Great Spirit can withdraw life and if a man interferes, he brings upon himself difficulties, pain and problems, by way of consequence – a living hell – and not just in one lifetime."

Wode became serious. "What I have told you is ancient knowledge from a sacred place. Nurture it within, and in years to come when the time is right and this has become your own immediate knowledge you can light up a mind, as I have in you. It is now woven into your destiny. Guard it well."

Wode looked deep into Geeter's eyes and Geeter found himself in no doubt of the importance of what he had just heard. There was a ripple of excitement in him: he knew that he'd been entrusted with a fragment of Life's great mysteries rising from the dawn of time. He was also aware of a feeling of rightness in him – a perfect moment like a key smoothly and easily turning a lock: the key of experience and knowledge unlocking the flow of karma deep within him.

---

As Wode predicted, they reached the Tulrain River in the middle of the day and stopped for lunch before making the crossing. They sat on a fallen tree, taking in the wide views across the plain from a mound above the river. Swallows, the acrobats of the skies, dived hither and thither in wide swooping arcs, catching unwary flies in hungry beaks; families of ducks bobbed about close to the banks, pulling at the abundant vegetation; and the sporadic flash of kingfisher blue, as they fired their little bodies like arrows into the clear waters, to re-emerge with a wriggling sliver of silver. The Tulrain was quite fordable at this point and over the years fore-thinking folk had dropped small rocks into the river to continue the road, so that it stretched into the wide flowing waters and emerged, refreshed and new, on the other side. The banks were largely open, swathed in grasses and wild flowers, and dotted with small clumps of trees, where their seeds had been carried downstream and dropped by previous floods, to begin a life.

When it was time to cross, the horses took to the clear water without fuss and happily picked their way across the pebbly bottom and up the far west bank, bringing their riders ever closer to Tulkney and the meeting with Geeter's mother.

"The last time I crossed this river," said Geeter, "I was hitching a ride with a caravan of traders from Woulin. They were a kind lot, rowdy too, and told good stories of their travels. They told me how important their nomadic trading was for them to earn money, and to return home to their families as wealthy as they could. On their outward journeys they felt safe and easy but as they exchanged their goods for money, they gradually became wary and on the look-out for wayside thieves and robbers.

"I remember an old man with a long white beard who was on his last trip. He was asking me what I wanted to do with my life. He had had a good run, he said, but he warned me off the life of a travelling trader with a story about a merchant who had spent all his life building as big a fortune as he could; he lived in a fine house and his family had all the luxuries they could wish for – do you know this one?"

"I don't think so, Geeter. Tell on."

"Well, if I remember rightly…One day he was visited by the messenger of death, who told him his time had come. He pleaded with him, saying he had much to do in his life still, but the messenger was not impressed. He promised him a third of his wealth and the messenger just shook his head. He promised half of his wealth if he would give him a few more months of life and still death's messenger said no. Finally the merchant said, 'I will give you all of my wealth if you will give me a few days with my family.' And the messenger replied, 'There is nothing you can give me that can change things, but I will grant you five minutes to write a letter.' And so the merchant reached for some fine parchment and he wrote a few lines before collapsing. His family found him with the quill still in his hand and his head laid beside his parting words. They read: 'I devoted my life to making a fortune and in the end it couldn't buy me what truly mattered – time with my beloved family. Time with those that you love is the real fortune of life. Use your time wisely, for it doesn't come around again.'"

"Wise words, indeed Geeter; it is hard for those who must make their living far from home. Have you been thinking about your mother?"

"Yes. I don't know what to do. I love my mother but I can't abide Sintle and yet I want to be with her, and also with you – learning to be a gnoseer."

"You will know in your heart what is right for you, Geeter. Your heart will inform you when the time is right, to do what you need to do." He looked across at his young friend astride Eska. He could see Geeter was reaching a small summit on his climb up destiny's mountain, and it was troubling him. Geeter glanced at Wode, seeking reassurance.

"Be easy. Spirit will show you the way by lighting the lantern in your heart. Thus it guides us all if only we would stop to see: if you ever feel you need to make an important decision, simply consult your heart's wisdom; just close your eyes and look, and see which way gives you the biggest 'yes'. You may be walking a road and come to a junction and you cannot see whether to turn left or right. Just close your eyes, let your inner wisdom rise in your heart to guide you and see which way – either the left or right – gives you the biggest 'yes'; out of ten it might feel to be four and a half for the left and five and a half for the right, and that is enough of a difference to give you the way to go. Right?"

Geeter nodded and fell silent. Wode could see he was concerned that, like all young people used to having parents telling them what to do, he would have no control over the outcome of the reunion with his mother.

"It is up to your mother, Geeter, but it is also up to you. You have your own life to lead, your own way to make, but your mother is your guardian until you can stand on your own two feet."

Geeter nodded and sighed, and Wode left him to his thoughts.

## Chapter 10

*A new beginning is but an end to what has gone before.*

They arrived in Tulkney late the following day. They were entering the town from the east, both gnoseer and boy tired after the long days on the road and anticipating a warm bed and good food. Wode had been keeping a wary eye on the big clouds coming in from the west, but no rain had fallen. He had seen this cloud build-up many times over the years at Brennan and he was expecting the big columns of grey to unleash their watery load and drench all beneath. For some reason their looming presence was making him uneasy.

Tulkney had been enjoying the tax parade: a day of thanksgiving and celebration for all those who contributed to the greater good. Those who had the ability to attract wealth through their gifts of commerce were proud to be recognised as contributing more financially than those whose gifts lay elsewhere. Such thanksgiving celebrations usually started with the parade and then continued into general merrymaking as shops and cellars were opened to celebrate everyone's place in society. Brackans knew that each individual had a unique spirit and contribution to make to the whole: some were gifted with animals and some were born to teach; others were inspiring listeners and lightened a burdened soul; some were good storytellers and entertained; big men gave of their physical strength; others were born to lead, to organise, and there were those who enhanced this flair for leadership by playing supporting roles. There were those who were gifted with plants and those whose talents lay in working with children. Brackans recognized that the gifts to mankind were endless and they all needed celebrating and acknowledging.

Wode and Geeter were greeted cheerfully as they went by. One or two came up to give them a drink or some food, which provided a welcome distraction for Geeter who was anxious about his mother's reaction to his homecoming, as she had quite a temper.

"Wode?"

"Yes?"

"My mother might blow up a fury when she sees me."

"Geeter, she's been longing for your return. There will be no fury."

"How can you be sure?"

"Gnoseers just know these things." Geeter was only partially reassured, his face tense with worry.

"What will happen?"

"She will open the door, glance at me and then run at you with open arms. She will hug you, you'll be half suffocated, I shall wait patiently, and then you will introduce me. At which point I will explain who I am and that I found you and persuaded you to return home. Then I will wend my way."

"Where will you go?" Concern wrinkling Geeter's forehead.

"I will stay with my friend Rintat a few days and if by then you have not joined me, I will continue on my journey. I will take Eska with me, as Rintat has a stable and some fields, until you decide what to do with her longer term."

"Where will your journey take you next?"

"One never knows," Wode said enigmatically, "but I shall probably head for Kuik," he heard himself say.

Deera lived at Kuik. Ever since they had met at the Wisdom Tree, Wode had found the image of her coming to him in his dreams. Sometimes only the briefest of flashes of her raven-black hair, her bright eyes or her departing back as she rode away. Last night, she had been standing atop a hill in flowing white robes, her long black hair streaming out behind her, flowing in the wind. He'd been transfixed by her smile and the sparkle in her deep green eyes, and felt compelled to climb the hill to reach her. But something was holding him back. He was aware the dream had meaning but now was not the time to dwell on it.

"How will I find you?" asked Geeter nervously.

"From where would you get the best view?"

Geeter smiled and looked upwards, scanning the sky. "From there?"

"Ask Keekra to keep me in sight. Rintat is the gnoseer in Tulkney and most people will know his house."

"All right," Geeter sighed. "Shall I show you where I live?"

"Yes, lead on."

The horses walked side by side up the wide streets of simple cottages. Geeter was keeping a wary eye – looking out for people who might know him. He really didn't want to be noticed. Finally he stopped under an oak tree beside a tidy, unassuming cottage with smoke trailing out of the chimney.

"This is it." Wode simply nodded and dismounted. He came round to hold Eska while Geeter slid hesitantly to the ground. He handed the reins to Wode in a trance of memories of bygone days and slowly moved towards the front door. Wode tied the horses to a post and watched Geeter walk forwards as though he were approaching a cliff edge, half expecting the ground to crumble beneath his feet.

"It'll be fine, Geeter," he said, putting his hand on his shoulder to reassure him for the final few steps. Troubled youngsters always found it hard to return to a home of painful memories. Geeter looked up at Wode. The recent confidence he had shown on the road seemed to have deserted him like a fickle friend.

"Take a deep breath, feel your feet connect to the earth, and knock," Wode commanded.

There was a pause and finally Geeter knocked. Nothing. He knocked again with more force. Movement could be heard inside and Geeter took a step back to await his mother's reaction. Footsteps approached the door and Geeter tensed as though unsure whether to stay or run. The door swung open to reveal a tired-looking woman haunted by her past. She was dark-haired with brown eyes that were accentuated by her pale skin.

"Hello, Mother."

"Geeter. Your ho…" She collapsed like a discarded cotton handkerchief, gently sinking to the ground. Wode strode past a stunned and confused Geeter, and picked her up carrying her into the house. He placed her gently on the fireside rug and pulled a chair over to support her feet, raising them from the ground.

"She's fine, Geeter, she's simply fainted in her shock at seeing you again." Wode was feeling for her pulse as he spoke and pressed a point beside her nose to revive her. She opened her eyes slowly and looked up at him.

"Who are you?"

"I'm a friend. I've brought Geeter home."

"Geeter," she called out. Falling on his knees beside her, he flung his arms around her in relief.

"I'm home, Mother, I'm home."

"Oh Geeter, I've missed you," tears welling in her dark eyes.

"I've missed you too," his tears combining with hers in a stream of happy reunion. Wode busied himself looking for honey. He found what he was looking for and placed a large dollop in the bottom of a cup and added hot water from a kettle beside the fire. He stirred the honey and brought the cup over to her.

"Can you sit?" He gently removed the chair from her feet and helped her into it, placing the warm honey drink into her grateful hands.

"Get that down you," he said kindly. She looked up slightly bewildered, and keeping her eyes on him, began to drink.

"My name is Wode and I am a gnoseer. I met Geeter on the road a half-moon or so ago and persuaded him to come home."

"I do thank you, Wode. My name is Heathra," and he inclined his head in acknowledgement.

"He's a good lad, Heathra. He was just troubled after your husband's death and the move here, and he needed to find something."

"What did you need to find?" Heathra turned to Geeter quizzically.

Wode continued on swiftly to keep her attention on him. "Answers to questions he did not know to ask; he needed to learn something about himself. He has talents, Heathra. Talents that could assist him to help others in his calling; talents that a gnoseer can see but are not perhaps so obvious to his parents. He has much to learn, but he has impressed me. And he has a question to ask you about his destiny and I suggest you give it serious consideration." She nodded blankly at his recommendation, his words slipping quietly into her subconscious to arise later to inform her.

"How are you feeling?"

"Stronger, thank you."

"Good. It can't have been easy for you these past months…" Heathra looked up at Geeter who was standing at her right shoulder.

"No, it hasn't been easy but I have seen that I made it very difficult for you, my lad," and she gripped his hand to reassure herself that he was real. She turned back to Wode. "To lose one's husband is a terrible, terrible thing but to lose one's child as well, is…" She shuddered. "Too awful."

Heathra put her hand around her son's waist and looked up into his eyes. "You came out of me. You are part of me." She looked away into the distance. "Yet I know we are destined to part; the young bird must fly his nest to make his way in the world, and that is right. But not today…" She trailed off into silence.

Geeter stood quietly by her side. Wode could see his energy changing; the haunted hole he'd been hiding was filling again at the delight of being reunited with his mother, and he was learning the consequences of his actions – the essence of experience. Wode was watching the situation minutely, judging the scene moment by moment. Her fainting had allowed her to be receptive to new information about her son and she was in a good place to see more, as long as Sintle did not return.

"Heathra, can I speak to you privately for a few minutes?"

"Yes of course."

"Geeter, go out to the back and call Keekra down to you."
Geeter nodded blankly and silently made his way out
through the back of the house and into the garden, where
he stood beside the vegetable beds, scanning the sky.

Wode moved to the parlour window overlooking the
back garden and turned to Heathra. "I'd like you to see
something before I leave. Just watch your son and notice
how assured he looks as he stands there…He's doing
something which only gnoseers know how to do."

Her face blended doubt and surprise in equal measure
as she joined him at the window. They stood in silence
watching Geeter, who with closed eyes stood still with
arms by his side.

"What's he doing?"

"He's reaching out."

"Reaching out? To what?"

"Just give it a few more minutes." Wode studied Geeter
to check he was calm inside. Satisfied, he looked up to
scan the sky. Instinctively, Heathra looked up as well.

"Oh, there's a kite." She sounded faintly surprised.

"Mmm, a black kite – Geeter's favourite. Keep watching."

As they looked on from the house, Geeter slowly raised his arms and turned his head towards Keekra flying above. His whole body began to gently sway as he enjoyed himself with his feathered companion. After some minutes he stood still and simply raised his right arm. Keekra swooped down, braking her glide to alight effortlessly on his forearm.

"Goodness! Did the kite come with you?"

"In a way."

"His father was a falconer, you know."

"Yes, but she's a wild bird and Geeter can call her without having to draw her with food. And he can use her eyes to see through."

"Are you sure?" Heathra tried not to look doubtful, even at the words from a gnoseer.

Wode nodded. "Do you remember him telling you about his flying dreams when he was younger?"

"Yes, but I just thought those were the silly dreams of a child." She looked slightly defensive and Wode could see he was losing her a little.

"No dreams are silly to a child. Children can see things most adults cannot because they are still in touch with the magic in Spirit. Adults tend to lose it; most of a gnoseer's training is learning where the barriers of experience have pushed out what we knew in early childhood."

Heathra said nothing and turned to watch Geeter talking to the bird on his arm; he was rapidly becoming aware of Keekra's grip on his poorly protected sleeve and he launched her heavenwards. She saw Geeter close his eyes, smiling as he did so.

"He's connecting to her now and seeing what she sees."

Heathra's doubt kept her silent as she watched her son. She didn't want to challenge the man who had returned her firstborn to her. The kite was out of sight and so she simply stood watching her son, enjoying what she thought she'd never see again. She noticed the changes in him; he looked older, stronger, more settled within himself. Perhaps his journey has helped him, she thought.

Suddenly Heathra saw Geeter frown and look panicked. "I've got to go," she heard him call out as he turned to make his way back towards the house. Wode knew exactly what had happened.

Geeter came into the room looking agitated, the confidence and poise he'd shown in the garden melting like snow in warm sunshine.

"Sintle's coming. I've just seen him pass the baker's. He'll be here soon."

Wode turned to Heathra, smiling. "And how would he have known that?"

"I don't know." She realised the gnoseer had been telling the truth.

"Presumably Sintle has been joining in the parade celebrations?" Wode continued.

"Yes. I didn't feel I had anything to celebrate."

"Quite so." Wode nodded towards Geeter. "Is Sintle a happy drunk?"

"Yes, don't worry. He won't be pleased to see him but he'll be relieved for me."

Wode considered for a moment and decided he could leave. "Right. I will go now and look out my old friend Rintat." He looked at Geeter. "Come on, Geeter, let's get your things." He reached the door and looked back at Geeter's mother. "You have a son to be proud of, Heathra. Listen to him."

"Thank you, Wode. And thank you again for bringing him home safely."

"It was my pleasure. Farewell." Wode smiled and left.

"Goodbye."

Wode led the way out to the tethered horses. Geeter followed, suddenly aware of the significance of their parting. Wode handed down the pack from Eska's back, seeing Geeter's concern spreading across his face. He had left to get away from Sintle and his mother, not to run towards a known opportunity. His mind had been reassured by the simple plan, and the longer he'd stayed on the road, the more he felt it was right. Now he was back at his starting point, and the old wounds seemed to be about to open again.

Wode gripped Geeter's shoulder firmly and looked deep into his eyes. "Life knows what you need, Geeter. You're stronger than you know. All will be well." He saw a flicker of reassurance in the youngster's eyes.

"We've had quite a journey, you and I," Wode continued, smiling. "Now go and face your past. Remember, you are stronger than you know, you have lived a hundred lives or more and faced circumstances far worse. You have hidden depths of knowledge gathered from this life and beyond; it is only your current youth that is showing you limits. They are not real – only imagined obstacles. Put uncertainty to the sword!"

Geeter nodded, hesitated, and then buried his face in Wode's chest, squeezing as hard as he could until Wode winced. He hugged him for all the good times he'd spent with his fatherly mentor, for hope for the future and for the strength to face his mother and Sintle together. He let go suddenly, smiled tearfully up at Wode and then went to find his mother.

"And remember, by seeing Sintle on his way home, you have just demonstrated your ability with birds to your mother. She was watching you."

Geeter stopped, half turned and nodded as the significance of Wode's words reached him.

Wode watched his departing back, feeling a surprising sense of sadness well up in his chest – the loss of Mara and his son and now his departing young friend. He shook his head, ruefully gathering himself, and untied the horses. "Karma is karma," he muttered and led his four-legged companions off towards Rintat's house. It began to rain.

---

Rintat was pleased to see his young friend. He was an old man now, complete with long white hair and beard, and twinkling eyes. Like most gnoseers, he had a particular talent that gave him more power with that gift than others. Rintat's unique gift was that of healing, and he had been especially diligent in passing his knowledge on to Wode when he was doing his apprenticeship time with him. Most gnoseers could heal what people brought to them but, if there was something that they could not resolve, they sent for Rintat. However, most of the time Rintat stayed where he was. The summons was telepathic and he would pick up the request and tune into the one in need of healing. Wode had been a favourite apprentice, largely because he was so adept himself already, and Worian had sent Wode to study with him, recognising that his talent required tuition far greater than even Worian could provide.

They spent three days together with much laughter, as Rintat was an exceptional storyteller, and that was what he recognised Wode needed. Like most gnoseers who knew him, he sensed soon after Wode's wife and child had died what Wode had gone through, and he also expected him to solrom and find his way to him in Tulkney. He was fascinated with the way his journey had unfolded and was pleased to hear how some of the skills he'd taught his younger protégé had been put to use. Wode enjoyed Rintat's healing talk and allowed himself to be counselled and helped with the hardness he felt that was the kernel of his grief. In return, the younger man gave him the company of an equal – a rare pleasure – and helped him with all manner of chores that the older man was unable to complete.

The rain had kept them indoors a lot of the time, with short trips to the hencoop or the barn to milk and feed the goat or make good the repairs needed around the home. Although Wode had his quiet, studious side he was more of an outdoorsman, and on the evening of the second day Rintat recognised a restlessness in Wode that was not just from being confined to the house.

"It does not look like your young friend is coming; have you tuned in and tracked him?"

"No," Wode admitted, "I did not want to interfere with his karma."

"You are a stickler. Have you considered that his karma might require you to tune in?"

"The right thing is not to interfere."

"It does not do any harm to bend the rules a little." Rintat's big, brown, owl-like eyes twinkled in the candlelight. "Karma is fluid, after all."

"Mmm. But this really should come from him."

"Fair enough, my friend. Fair enough. As long as it is not pride." He got slowly to his feet. "Well, I am totally floomered! It's time for this old body to unfloom."

"Floomered? Is that one of your new words, Rin?"

"Yes. I'll leave you my word book in my will," he chuckled and left the room, anticipating a good night's sleep. Wode sat smiling to himself as he watched the flames dancing in the fire; he'd not told Rintat about reaching out to Sintle.

———

The following morning Wode awoke to the sounds of Rintat coughing and moving about the house, and joined him outside feeding the hens.

"The rain is staying over the upper highlands by the look of it," said Wode.

"Yes, but at least it has stopped here. How is the young fellow?"

"My sense is that he is fine."

"Fine to stay or fine to join you?"

"His heart is enjoying being reunited with his mother."

"Mmm, not surprising really. He is young."

"Yes. I'd have enjoyed having him as an apprentice, but his destiny is his own to follow, and anyway I cannot stay, I have been called to the Tree again."

"Again? Really?" Rintat's eyebrows shot up his forehead in surprise. "That will be twice within one moon-cycle. That is unusual, very unusual. It has never happened to me…yet. This must be about you."

"Mmm, as the ancient lore has it. Perhaps there are exceptions, or the bigger karmic picture is changing."

"Well, let us enjoy a big breakfast and then you can prepare yourself some provisions for the journey. I will look after Geeter's horse."

"Thank you, Rin."

They moved inside and starting preparing food; however Rintat could see that Wode was keen to get going. "Why the impatience?"

"The pull to the Tree is really strong, in fact I have never had it so strong." Wode tapped his chest. "And if it is about me, I'd rather get to it and meet my fate head on."

"You had better eat on the road. Go on and get Tarn saddled up and I will finish something here for you."

Wode nodded, deep in thought, and went off to find Tarn. He soon returned with her saddled and ready and went inside to find his pack. Rintat joined him as he was securing it to the saddle.

"Here is some food. I have had this old saddlebag for years and never use it, so take it; I have put your breakfast in the left side and the rest to be going on with on the right." And with that he swung it over Tarn's neck and secured it.

"Thank you, Rin. It's been good to see you. You know you have helped me. I am leaving lighter. Thank you."

Wode's friend looked him in the eye. "You will find the grief almost gone now, you can be free but…" He hesitated. "Don't take any daft risks."

Wode looked at him, assessing his words, and simply nodded. He embraced his friend farewell. "Thanks, Rin. I'll be fine, don't you worry."

He mounted, waved and turned Tarn towards the road, calling over his shoulder, "I will see you on my way back."

"'Till then, Wode of Brennan. Farewell," Rintat called out, watching his friend trot off. "Fare thee well," he murmured, concerned.

———————

Late afternoon on the following day Wode reached the banks of the Tulrain again. The river was born high up in the highland mountains to the north and was joined by many streams and smaller rivers by the time it turned south in the great central basin. With heavy rain in the hills over the past days, the river was flowing fast and strong, deep and peaty, and it was impossible to see the riverbed beyond a few feet in. As he approached the fording point a man was just emerging from the river on horseback.

"How is it?" enquired Wode.

"Fast and deep – too much for me. I'd wait it out if I were you."

"Do you know the ford well?"

"Aye, I use it a lot."

"What is the best line?"

"Well if you have to go, keep your line on that old alder on the other side; if you stray too far, it gets too deep and you'll have to get off and allow the horse to swim. Especially this side, where the river bends towards us."

"Thank you." The man nodded in acknowledgement and went off to wait.

Wode spent some time studying the water, getting a sense of it. He was sure the water was dropping, albeit slowly, and so he bided his time, eating the remainder of the bread Rintat had given him. Yet the longer he waited the more he was aware of the call to the Tree, a pull unusually strong in the centre of his chest. Wode even considered he was mistaken and was experiencing some form of illness, but he looked inside and couldn't discern anything amiss in his energy field. Finally he started pacing and looking to see which was the biggest yes — to go now or wait still further. His intuition was not giving him anything and he couldn't see what to do, and so he did nothing. And still the pulling in his chest persisted, until finally his impatience got the better of him. A calling is a calling after all, he reasoned, and he mounted.

"Are you ready for this, Tarn?" She flickered her ears.

"Good girl." He stroked her neck and scratched her between the ears. "Take it nice and easy and we will be fine. We can both swim if necessary." Her head came round to look at him, as though she were not in the slightest bit reassured.

Wode nudged Tarn forward. She was tentative so he patted her neck and talked to her in soothing tones as she edged forward. He could tell she was frightened but she kept going. He knew some horses simply didn't like not being able to see the ground in front of them. The current was pulling at his feet as further and further they went, ever so slowly into the fast-flowing river. Tarn was as tense as a bowstring.

"Good girl Tarn, you're doing fine. Keep going." Reassured by his voice, she continued to edge slowly forward, further into the roaring water. He patted her neck and, staring ahead, leant forward to be closer to her right ear so that she could hear him gently coaxing her on; yet it meant he was oblivious to what was coming towards them, driven by the extra current coming off the bend.

The sound of water was loud in his ears but he could just make out a shout. He looked up to follow the sound: a man was on the far bank, pointing upstream. Wode turned to look and saw a tree, roots to branches, bearing down on them in the fast current. Wode felt a prickle of fear. Rintat's words echoing around his head, "Don't take any daft risks." Tarn shuddered beneath him – she had seen it too and was beginning to panic, thrashing around as if to unseat him.

Time to swim, he thought as Tarn stumbled, suddenly losing her footing in the strong current, and immediately he realised he should have entered the water with feet out of the stirrups. Tarn went down hard on her left side as he tried to disengage his feet and dismount. Losing his balance he fell forward onto her neck. Feeling his weight on her neck, Tarn thrashed about the more, panic giving her wild strength, and with his right foot suddenly free, he was thrown upstream to be immediately swept back into her belly, fuelling her panic still further. Through the thrashing legs and swirling water, Wode fought for the surface with his left foot trapped, his head breaking free long enough to gasp a breath before going down again. Tarn stopped thrashing as she lost contact with the rocky bed and was forced to swim, and Wode was able to surface again and get a look at the opposite bank. Too far, he thought, before being dragged under again as he frantically fought to free his foot.

Tarn suddenly turned downstream, trying to swim away from the tree. Wode's body was caught by the powerful current and swept round under her neck. The next time he surfaced, he was beside the horse's head and facing the near bank he'd just left. Through blinking eyes he momentarily glimpsed figures on the bank shouting and waving at him before being dragged under the surface again. Tarn's knees kept pushing him down, winding him; lungs bursting, he was fighting the body's panic, frantically reaching for the surface and then finally he was up again, gulping lungfuls of sweet air. Foot horribly twisted. Knife, he thought, and reached for his knife to cut the stirrup… He tried again to pull himself round against the current to release his foot but he was tiring fast and gave up and fought desperately again for the surface. Suddenly Tarn stopped struggling and he was able to release his foot as he surfaced. He only just managed to fill his lungs before the tree hit him.

Those watching on the bank saw one of the revolving branches hit Wode. The tree was rotating slowly in the current like a mill wheel and his limp body, caught up in the branch, was slowly raised out of the water and swept downstream for thirty yards to the apex of the bend. Here the tree came to an uncertain, teetering halt, at any moment to continue its journey downstream on the boiling, swirling current that was tirelessly urging it on.

Wode was in blackness, a deep penetrating black fatigue, weighing down every fibre of his being until he could hold on no more, and he let go. Simple. Released, he drifted to float imperceptibly through an invisible doorway and he smiled as a distant light beckoned. It was beautiful, the most wonderful light he had ever seen. He was utterly content – released – fatigue vanishing into eternity. So light and free, and he could see…Mara! "My love." He realised he wasn't speaking and yet could communicate words and thoughts with the greatest of ease. Then he was floating and looking down at his body. A man was pulling it up the bank; there was something familiar about him. He was fascinated by this end scene. Warmth. He turned back to the light. "Mara, my love, I've missed you." She waved and moved towards him. They entwined. "I've missed you, Mara."

"But I've always been with you." She smiled. He felt the ecstasy of their love — stronger than ever. It filled him completely; the power running through him; he felt immortal. Mara spoke: "I live in your heart. You know so much about life yet you forget in your grief where your love is."

"You are my love." She smiled at his words. "It's not me you love. It's the immortal spirit in woman. You must go back and make this love real again in your life."

"But I want you."

"And you shall have me, for I am the spirit in every woman if you can only love enough, and then we will be united for all eternity. I promise you." She reached out a golden hand towards his chest. He felt warmth entering him. Flowing swiftly, filling his body. She began to move away, smiling, glowing. He began to fall; falling… falling… voices. He heard her calling his name but she was far off now.

"Wode… Wode…" Falling and falling, she was receding back towards the Light. Gone.

"Wode… Wode." He coughed, and groaning, rolled over and coughed some more.

"Wode!" He rolled back towards the voice. He felt his head being lifted and warmth underneath.

"Wode," said a soft, loving voice. He knew the voice, a joyous recognition. He opened his eyes. He blinked in the light and smiled. His hand reached unsteadily up to the beautiful, newly familiar face that leant over him. She held his hand against her cheek and he smiled into her large, beautiful eyes. They were deep green, beside long raven hair.

"Thank you for coming back," she said.

"Thank you for giving me reason to."

## Chapter 11

*An end is but a new beginning by another name.*

Once again Wode stood atop one of the few hills rising out of the Tulrain basin, looking out over the rich, fertile grasslands reaching south to merge with the sky on the southern horizon. The surrounding hills merged seamlessly into the wide flat plain at their feet and were covered in legions of fir, beach and oak – in places like a thick green woodland sauce flowing onto the grassland below. He was standing in a clearing above a sharp drop surrounded by oak – narrower in the trunk but taller than their cousins that grew in open pastureland. The sun's heat was warming his chest as he enjoyed the wide vista again.

Having crossed the river, the road had kept beside the diminishing floodwaters until it came to a long gorge between two hills that appeared to remain upstanding after the rest of the valley had dropped down in a long-forgotten seismic shift. The road skirted around the base of the eastern hill on which he was now surveying the wide valley. Wode turned to look behind him as Harrell and Deera dismounted and joined him to bask in the breathtaking beauty that lay at the heart of Bracka.

"The backbone of Bracka – it is beautiful, isn't it?" Wode ventured. Deera turned to smile up at him, her large green eyes holding his gaze.

"I've never seen it from this side before. It is beautiful, as you say."

Harrell said nothing and simply allowed his eyes to rove the distances, following the flight of a distant pair of eagles making the most of the rising thermals where the ground rose sharply off the valley floor.

"And you can see the Wisdom Tree," he said, pointing. "Over there, outstanding all around."

"It is colossal, isn't it?" Harrell agreed.

They were silent again; stilled in the beauty they felt within, reflected from the fertile beauty without.

"There is a spring close by and so I often camp up here. I would like to get an early night and set off at dawn tomorrow. I will show you where is best."

"Sounds good to me," Harrell said.

Wode led Tarn a short way to stand under a single large beech and pulled his pack down from her back, followed by the saddle. He dropped her reins to the ground.

"Stay close, Tarn, and keep an eye on the other two." She looked at him as if he were insulting her intelligence. He patted her rump affectionately and went to help Deera with her pack and saddle.

"Thank you, kind sir." She flashed him a smile that melted into him. "I will prepare some food if you get the fire going."

Wode puffed out his chest. "Man make fire," he joked and went off, feeling slightly foolish, to find some kindling sticks.

Within fifteen minutes he had small flames jumping skywards and Harrell brought some larger sticks to sustain the fire for the night. There was an easiness between them all as they settled around the warming glow, invisible bonds of shared experience – the river drama and travelling the same road together.

It was Harrell who had hauled Wode off the tree caught precariously in the bend in the river. He had stayed long enough to see Wode wake up and recognise Deera, before running down the bank to reach Tarn. The panicked horse was frantically trying to climb up a steep part of the bank. Harrell had jumped into the shallows beside her and had led her to a gentler incline some thirty yards downstream. She tried to bolt on reaching flat ground but he had held on, walking her round and round, talking to her quietly until she calmed down. He'd then brought her over to be reunited with Wode.

Deera and Harrell had left Tulkney a day before him, travelling at a slower pace. They had been camped – set back hidden from the road in a forest clearing near the river when Wode would have passed. Harrell's relatives had wanted to see them off at the river and had driven a wagon from Tulkney with tents and provisions aplenty, to make an expedition of it.

Wet and exhausted, Wode had walked back with them to the camp they'd made the previous night, and once warm and dry, he had fallen into a deep restorative sleep that lasted right through to the following morning.

Up early the next day, he was not only famished but keen to get across the river and down the Tulrain valley to the Wisdom Tree. As they'd breakfasted he'd told Deera and Harrell about why it was that he was journeying from Tulkney. As the Wisdom Tree was on their way home, he had suggested they continue their journey together.

———————

Lying by the fire, they were enjoying the sense of peace that follows a good meal; a comfortable stillness. Their supper had been simple and delicious and their bodies were grateful for the sustenance after a long day in the saddle. Wode looked over and studied Harrell's face while he gazed into the fire. The warm glow revealed a broad, kind face used to being in authority over others and behind that, there was something…a sadness…a lack of…Wode closed his eyes and reached out to his companion. When he opened them again, Harrell was looking at him.

"What is your passion, Harrell, apart from your work or family?"

Harrell shifted slightly and looked off into the distance. "Horses. I have a passion for horses." He sighed. "I love everything about them – their beauty, the grace of their movement; their proud, independent nature; their spirit – and they appear to respond to me instinctively; I seem to know their character intuitively." He smiled. "Why do you ask?"

"Well, if I may speak freely?" Harrell nodded. "I sense a lack of fulfilment in you. There's something missing for you. Your life is fine and comfortable of course, but it isn't reaching you, not as deeply as it could. You have an air of a man who would rather be doing something else but is caught up in his day-to-day existence, such that he feels he cannot change the status quo. Wouldn't you rather let go of the cloth trading and be breeding horses?"

Deera was nodding. "Yes, he would, he seems to glow when he is with his horses." Harrell looked surprised at his daughter's comment – like many people, he thought he was more difficult to read.

"Well why don't you?" Wode continued.

Harrell grew pensive, exploring a new sensation in him – as though the lock on a large forgotten closed door, deep within the bowels of a castle, had magically been released;

a secret to which he'd provided safe haven was released to fly – to live. He half smiled, not used to this personal a conversation with someone other than his wife.

"I need to continue to run the trading house until my son is ready, and I'm not sure Aruna would support the idea."

"How old is he?" Wode asked gently.

"Father! Tolban is twenty-eight. He's a bright and capable man." Deera's frustration got the better of her. She loved her father but his paternal protectiveness could be stifling.

Wode smiled at them. "So he's old enough! And if you spoke from your heart to reveal your passion for horses to Aruna, I am sure she would want to share that life-change with you. I think she is bored but doesn't know it, and if you get a new lease of life, well, she's going to enjoy your new passion."

They both looked at Wode in surprise. Harrell hesitated. "I had thought the same only recently but not wanted to ask her for fear she might be bored with me."

Wode was touched by Harrell's admission. "It is not you, but find your passion in everything you do and she will never be bored."

Harrell nodded pensively. "I'll talk to her when I return."
He stared into the fire for a few minutes, his eyes gleaming
with the light of new possibilities. "Time for my bed," he
said, and pulled his blanket about him, wriggling this way
and that to get comfortable. Finally, pulling his blanket
up over his shoulders, he sighed contentedly and was still.
"Goodnight," he called out.

"Goodnight," they chorused and sat listening to the
embers crackle and the sounds of the night as they stared
into the dancing flames. Deera was first to speak.

"Have you ever missed a calling to the Tree?"

"This time was the closest," he said ruefully. "No, gnoseers
always get there. I've never heard of anyone not making it."

"And you were called very recently for my question; is it
common to be called again so soon?"

"No. It's not usual." He looked at her to see if she was
leading up to something. "If you get called again so soon,
it has always been due to the predestined karma of the
gnoseer."

"But don't you wise and all-knowing gnoseers know this
– what your karma is?" Deera was teasing him slightly,
much to his delight, but he pretended to be serious.

"Much of our predestined karma is beyond our individual reach, otherwise we would not get the pleasure of the surprise." She smiled. Her intuition told her that they were destined to spend time together; why else would Life have arranged such a dramatic reunion for them?

"I see. And so why do you think you nearly drowned?" She was enjoying herself.

"Well, er…"

The years of living seemed to melt away to reveal a young boyish face.

Wode took a deep breath and, feeling slightly giddy, jumped into the fire of his burgeoning love. "Well, to meet you again of course."

A woman loves to be acknowledged by a man she is attracted to. Deera smiled at him demurely. "Well you went to some pretty dramatic lengths to get my attention."

He laughed. "Yes, well…it worked," and flashed her a smile full of youthful bravado. She beamed back at him in shared understanding and promise. Such a look from a woman can ignite a fire in a man that sustains his spirit through the hardest of times; the knight rises. Dreaming of her, the fire blazes, torturing his heart with yearning;

left alone it glows in his depths, quietly leading him to that promise of love with his princess.

"And what of Geeter?"

"Well, it seems he is staying in Tulkney with his mother after all. I have not sensed anything different."

Wode had been distracted by his recovery from near drowning, the calling to the Wisdom Tree and of course the presence of the lovely Deera.

"Perhaps I will send Geeter a message after I am done at the Tree."

"What do you mean?"

"A gnoseer's journeying. Simply go still inside, like you saw me do at the Tree last time, and reach out to him through the inner realm that we are all connected to. I can get a sense of how he is, and if necessary send a dream message to him."

"You would have liked to have taken him on, wouldn't you?"

"Yes I would. I have to pass on my knowledge to at least one other. It ensures the balance of things. And he would have been a good candidate: bright, self-reliant and pretty fearless. And he's gifted…"

"I'd have liked to have met him."

"You would like him."

"I'm sure." Deera yawned and suddenly looked tired. "It's been another long day; if you'll excuse me I think I'll put my head down too." She smiled across at him. "Goodnight, Wode."

"Goodnight, Deera, thank you for supper."

"My pleasure." And with that she closed her eyes and reflected on their conversation. She smiled at the ease of their companionship, how they were drawn together by karma to the Wisdom Tree and how the calling to the Tree had drawn them together again. Since Beam, Wode was the first man with whom she'd felt a connection. He was different, quiet, without a need to impress, and she could see how some might interpret that as aloofness; yet his smile was warm, coming from a love and compassion for his fellow man and woman, and although he took his calling seriously, he took himself lightly. As she thought of him, she wriggled inside with delight, a small ripple of enjoyment bubbling up from the depths of her —

love's immortal hope. She knew that sharing a traumatic experience with someone forged a bond beneath personality, a sacred connection of souls. She recalled cradling his head on the riverbank; there was something...

"Wode?"

"Yes, Deera?"

"On the riverbank..."

"Mmm?"

"Did you cross the threshold of this world?"

"Yes I did."

She turned to face him, propping herself up on one elbow. "You looked at peace...Would you tell me what you saw?"

He hesitated, like any wise man about to mention a past love to a potential mate. "Well...I saw Mara."

"Oh." She'd not been expecting that. The ripple of hope dying in her belly. "What happened?"

"She taught me something..." Wode paused, opening like a dormant bud that had missed a thousand springs;

the depth of his recent grief had cracked the ice, but Deera's attention and presence warmed a path for his emerging words to be known. "She showed me there is one eternal female Spirit that lights every woman's soul, and it is that light that we men truly love. With this knowledge she showed me I could love again."

"Ohhh." She felt her cheeks flush as his words lit the fire which fuelled every woman's hope for love. She had really not been expecting that.

She had her answer. "Thank you, Wode, goodnight."

"Sleep well, Deera." Wode drew his shieldagh down over Harrell and Deera, and then over himself. He remained awake awhile, listening to the sounds of the night, pondering on the changes in him, and on his good karma – bringing a beautiful woman into his life. "Thank you, Great Spirit, a lovely choice." An owl hooted in the distance. He followed it awhile before easing over into contented sleep.

---

They awoke at dawn and quietly prepared for their onward journey. Breakfast consisted of thick biscuits and honey, washed downed with hot sweet tea. Ready to mount, Wode gave Deera a leg-up into her saddle and received a warm smile of thanks. They started down the hill, the horses carefully picking their way down the steep slope and onto the lush green of the plain below. The hooves of the horses began to glisten gold as, moistened by the dew, they caught the light of the sun cresting the hills to the east. It cast its warmth and golden brightness over the vast expanse of plains grasses, coaxing them into a brighter green than the early dawn sky; no blade of grass was forgotten by this kiss of morning light.

The higher the sun rose, the quicker their pace seemed to become. Wode was acutely aware of the pull in his chest; the call to the Tree was strong and he wanted to keep the horses moving at a keen rate. Around mid-morning, they reached the fork in the road that led to the Tree and they halted to rest the horses and their backsides. They were sprawled out watching the procession of clouds across the vast sky. Harrell cleared his throat.

"Do you mind if I ask you, Wode, how you know that your presence is required at the Wisdom Tree?"

"Not at all. I usually have a dream and see the Tree without a Keeper, and in that way I know it is my watch. There is also a pulling in my chest, here…" He got up and walked over to where Harrell was sitting and knelt beside him, putting his hand in front of Harrell's chest about three inches from his heart. "Can you feel that?"

There was a pause. "Uw, yes. It's like you are trying to pull my heart out of my ribcage. That's very strange."

Wode grinned at him. "I have had that for several days now. And you can see why we would want to get rid of that feeling."

"Goodness, that could drive you to drink. And it goes when you get there?"

"Within a few hundred yards of the Tree, the sensation spreads out and fills the chest – it turns to a sort of lifting, mild excitement."

"Well, well."

Wode remained standing, resigned. "It is time for me to go now."

He looked down at Deera, who raised her hand for him to help her up. He pulled her gently at first and then with more force through the arc of her balance, so that she couldn't stop herself falling into his waiting arms, and he hugged her.

He pulled away and looked at her at arm's length. "Thank you, Deera." She knew what he meant.

He glanced at Harrell and then looked deep into Deera's eyes. "I would like to visit you in Kuik when I am finished here. Would that sit well with you?"

Wode looked back at Harrell, who nodded, smiling.

Deera spoke, a slight huskiness betraying her emotion. "I would like that, Wode." Her smile swelled his heart and they embraced with a longing for the next time. Pulling away, Wode bent over, reaching into his pack and rummaging a little before withdrawing a beautiful white crystal the size of his thumb. He placed it in her hand and, cupping both his hands around hers, he spoke a few words quietly and then let go.

"I'll know where to find you now."

She opened her hands. "Thank you, Wode, it's beautiful."

"Don't leave it too long," said Harrell, rising to his feet.

"I won't, and thank you." Wode looked him in the eye. "Enjoy your horses."

"I will, young Wode. I will. Until the next time," and clasped him by the hand.

Wode mounted, waved and nudged Tarn into a trot. A hundred yards on, he turned to wave to Deera. She waved eagerly back, sending his heart soaring like an eagle in full splendour. He nudged Tarn in the ribs to pick up speed; the sooner he left, the sooner he could see her again.

----

Wode reached the Wisdom Tree in the mid-afternoon. The sun was bright on the western side and the flowers were releasing their sweet perfume of abundant nectar; bees, butterflies and hoverflies were dancing in attendance from flower to flower.

As Wode drew up, a man unfamiliar to him came out from under the Tree. The first thing he noticed about him was his long straight nose above a wide smile. He was short and wiry, and reminded Wode of a happy ferret. He warmed to him immediately and dismounted.

"Greetings, I'm Wode of Brennan."

"Greetings to you. Lorrick of Corthairn."

"Corthairn, is that Uik way?"

"That's right, a fair way indeed."

"In both senses of the word," he agreed. "Will you stay the night or are you needing to go?"

"I'd be keen to stay. Some company would be refreshing and then I could get a good start tomorrow."

"Very good. I'll see to my horse and then join you."

Wode took off his saddle and pack, and led Tarn down to the stream to get her fill of cool, clear water. When she started pulling at the flowers lining the bank he lifted her head and led her back towards the Tree. Close enough to keep her in sight, he dropped the reins and left her to pull at the nourishing carpet of grass, and he joined his new friend in some tea, fresh from the big Tree's flowers.

They passed the evening sharing food and stories, comparing the situations they were called to in their locale, their visits to the Tree and the questioners they'd met, and as always when gnoseers got together they talked of their sense of the state of the collective karma. Something was shifting, they agreed, a shadow was forming like storm clouds way off over the ocean, but it was too early to name the cause and, therefore, the remedy. It would be a matter for the Gnoseers' Gathering at some time in the future.

The Gnoseers' Gathering was a council of the gnoseer elders that took place once a year, in a hidden valley on the east side of the southern highlands, relatively close to the centre of Bracka. It was a curious gathering, with a history stretching back to the beginning of time, and often included those who could not be there, yet who attended in Spirit form or animal form – usually as a bird – to cover the distances needed to travel. It was a gathering that monitored the state of Bracka's spirit and collective karma, and due to the gathering of powerful beings present, energy could be directed to where it was needed most, in times of trouble. It was incredible to behold for the first time – something gnoseers never forgot and never spoke about to anyone save those apprentices who were ready to witness this mystical gathering of those who practised the ancient ways, and carried their secret forward into the future for the good of all.

Tired from his travels, Wode called it a night soon after dark and went off to find his favourite cocoon of root branches to sleep in. Once he was settled into his niche, sleep came quickly, followed by dreaming – images rich and varied, stimulated no doubt by the conversation with Lorrick. Deera was waving at him from a boat and Geeter was flying with Keekra over Tulkney, dropping fruit on his mother.

---

Wode slept long and awoke to find Lorrick already up and packed, and ready to leave.

"Good morning, Lorrick, I trust I have not kept you."

"Good morning, and no, not at all. I've left some eggs by the fire for you and some fresh mushrooms, should you fancy. There is wood, enough for a day, I'd say. I'm just off to the stream to fill up with water and I'll be on my way."

"Right-ho." And with that Lorrick disappeared off to the stream, returning a few minutes later to find Wode making tea.

"Have you time for a cup?"

"No thank you, I'm keen to put in some distance. I have not seen the family for a few weeks."

"I understand. Journey well, and do look me up in Brennan, should you be over our way."

"I will, my friend."

They clasped hands briefly and then Lorrick was gone. Wode watched his departing back and then returned to his tea. He was grateful to be alone again and felt a deep inner peace. He smiled to himself, stretched and then set about the day.

---

After a simple lunch, he left the shade of the great Tree and strolled aimlessly about, stopping to watch the birds darting in and out of the luxuriant foliage, enjoying their gentle twitter above a background of the humming insects that were calling on each of the Tree's small white flowers. He allowed his mind to idle in the soporific effect of the sun's warming rays.

For the first time in months he felt comfortable enough to think back, back to the darkest hours of his life…. He thought of Mara and their plans for a family being brought to a cruel finale, the agonising moments of despair and frustration at being helpless to intercede in her desperate demise. At the end as he cradled her in his arms – the all he could do – before her breath ceased for ever, she'd thanked him for his valiant efforts to save her, for the love they'd shared and in one last act of compassion, she'd told him to be open to love again. She'd spoken from a perspective above normal reality, that sacred place before passing over; she was seeing the gift and purpose of her life in its entirety, letting go with grace. He remembered the days afterwards, the kindness and love of all those in Brennan, the hollowness within like an empty tree – all bark and no core; the soul searching for meaning and perspective, and the eventual movement within to roam – soul roam.

His solrom: the peace of solitude as he journeyed like the dying notes of a beautiful solo, and he saw that in time others had combined with this song to bring a new melody that harmonised his heart. He smiled at the memory of meeting Geeter for the first time, knowing instantly that they were linked in an unfolding journey of karma, the stories already written within the pages of a great cosmic book. He saw how the boy had helped him out of his internal roaming, giving him purpose – his very presence demanding to be taught. How he reminded him of a more easy-going version of himself at that age; his parents had recognised that their son had an unusual sensitivity and he was presented to Agarth, the local gnoseer, for him to assess and suggest a course of destiny: he wasn't to be a carpenter like his father. Agarth already had an apprentice and he also recognised that the young Wode would need a more gifted gnoseer than he. And so he was sent away from his parents to study with Worian. Wode felt a pang of remembrance at the initial parting from his parents, for he was to be separated from them by many miles and eventually soaring levels of understanding, the very heights that Worian genially harnessed. Wode's mentor taught him well and endeavoured to lighten his rather serious young protégé; Wode could see Geeter's presence had lifted him, as had Deera's.

He stopped meandering a stone's throw from the Tree and stretched his long frame out in the full sun as his thoughts went to Deera. He'd never felt such an ease with another human being, not even Mara. Deera had a warmth that shimmered around her like a golden mirage; he couldn't imagine anyone not falling for her grace and simple beauty. He was in no way immune to her femininity, in fact he was powerless to resist her warm smile and sparkling eyes. As he lay there enjoying his reverie, suddenly a shard of guilt spliced his mood like a dark assassin – the thought that he shouldn't be thinking of another woman like this. And then almost immediately an image of Mara appeared to float in front of him, smiling encouragement, and the shadow of doubt left him like a skulking dog caught with hen feathers around its mouth; communication from the other realm was second nature to him and he was grateful for the ease of such contact.

Wode smiled at how the Great Spirit had brought Deera into his life in such a perfect way: she the questioner, he the gnoseer to answer her; both having plumbed the depths of grief and shared in the dramatic experience of his near drowning. Suddenly he was back on the riverbank. He saw with amazing clarity how his attempted crossing of the Tulrain River had led him into the death realm. He now knew the reality of death as an experience; it is the body that dies, the "I" doesn't, he said to himself. He'd known this intellectually, through his training, but having lived it, the essence of the experience was now part of him. Suddenly an invisible cosmic curtain parted and he was immediately aware of a new depth of peace in him; the subtle fear of dying in all animals that fuels their drive to survive had left him without trace. He was floating in the pure experience of being. Death had no fear. He had dropped into a lightness of joy he'd never known before: the joy of creation, as ageless as the universe itself. It had always been there, waiting to be discovered with a patience weighed in millennia. This was the first time his soul, in all its hundreds of lifetimes, over thousands of years, had experienced it. He floated in a sea of awe and mystery, closer than ever before to the knowledge of the blackness of the space between the stars...

He became aware of a vibration from the ground he was lying on and reluctantly he sat up. He could hear the sound of hooves pounding the earth, and judging by the rhythm, the horse was cantering. He knew this was his questioner and they seemed to be in a hurry. He slowly got to his feet to welcome the man or woman who was to have their question answered. I wonder what it is that is bringing this one to the Tree so fast, he thought. Over the years he'd had several eager ones, who'd travelled in haste to relieve the burning question that had consumed them for days or weeks, but this one – it looked like a woman – was not only in a hurry but appeared to be frantic, and was now waving and shouting.

Wode turned his head towards the wind, trying to pick up the woman's shouts. Is she warning of danger? Wode broadened his senses, sending them out wide to scan for any threat. Nothing.

Wode watched as the rider pushed the horse to go faster. She was now into a gallop. Goodness, she is in a hurry. Riding like a madwoman. Wode still couldn't quite hear the shouted words; he frowned and narrowed his eyes, trying to see more clearly. That's not a woman, that's a boy, he thought. Then the fog of uncertainty instantly cleared.

"Wode! Wode!"

Geeter?! His eyes widening in delight, laughter pouring out of him.

"And he's brought a whole flock!" Wode could now see, swirling this way and that, starlings, finches, sparrows and of course Keekra. Moments later Geeter was pulling Eska up hard, jumping down and running up to Wode for a hug.

"What are you doing here?" said Wode to the young head under his chin.

Geeter jumped back. "I've got a question for the Wisdom Tree!"

"So have I – what did your mother say?"

"She said she'd think about it, but it was Sintle who, on hearing I saw him through Keekra's eyes before he arrived back after the celebrations, said that he could never train me to be a tailor. He told her my mind would always be elsewhere and tailoring needed such precision. He also said that I had to find out if this really was my calling or just a passing fancy, having just met you, and the only way I'd know was to try it. But later, I was outside the house and Keekra suddenly swooped right down in front of me. So close, she brushed my nose!" Geeter was laughing and talking quickly.

"And then I started flying with Keekra and she told me I had to follow her. I kept asking her where and all she would tell me was 'far'. I went to see Rintat and he told me it was my destiny calling and to follow her. So I told my mother I had to go, saddled up Eska and followed."

"All the way here?"

"All the way here. Every day she'd lead me further and further away from Tulkney. It's very strange not knowing where you are going, just following a bird. I began to think I was going mad. And then I saw it. The Wisdom Tree! And I thought, My question! I can have my question answered about my future! Someone will be there for me to answer my question!" He was almost chanting in his excitement.

Wode was laughing. "Well I'm the only one here, so I must be the one to answer it. I'll just go and prepare."

"You don't need to do that. It's only a short question."

"Very well. So what is it?"

"Will you take me on as your apprentice?"

"Hmm. Now let me think about this."

"Please tell me you're joking!"

"The answer is… er…"

After the days of uncertainty, Geeter couldn't contain his not knowing. He started jumping and dancing for joy. "YES! It's yes! He said yes."

Over the years, Wode would pull Geeter's leg and remind him that he never actually answered the question; this was the first time a question had not been answered at the Wisdom Tree.

———————

# An Interview with Thomas Lawrence

*What was the first spark of inspiration for* Smiling the Moon?

Initially the idea was to write a self-help book based around the health and therapy work I do with clients and patients; I wanted to help more people than the one-to-one of my practice. But when I sat down to write, an image of a shaman-healer character walking a back-country road came to mind, and I simply began to put his story down on paper as it came to me.

*Had you done any writing before* Smiling the Moon, *and did the manuscript need much revision ahead of submission to the Writer's Workshop competition?*

I'd not written much previously, apart from press releases in a former job and an article for *The Big Issue*, and so yes, there was a great deal of hard work that went into making *Smiling the Moon* worthy of a submission to Hay House.

*Was there a specific inspiration, or inspirations, for the setting of the book?*

When I began writing *Smiling the Moon*, I was living and working in the Highlands of Scotland, a wonderful, mystical place of wild hills and hidden valleys, and this magical landscape certainly inspired a place in me where no one else had been: Bracka.

*What's your daily routine like when you're writing?*

A routine would be a luxury! My acupuncture and cognitive hypnotherapy practice mean that I don't work a 9–5 day, and so it's more of a question of finding an hour or two during 'admin time'. And if I'm feeling creative, I just sit at the keyboard with a cup of green tea and enjoy whatever comes to mind. But sometimes the urge to write comes when I'm out somewhere, and so I just find a pen and some paper and begin that way.

*What challenges did you face in bringing the book to life?*

Time, time and time. I had so much to learn about the storytelling process, and how to bring what I could see in my head out onto the page in a way that others could see, and hopefully enjoy. It simply took a lot of hours and days, and I'm a bit of a perfectionist so would go over paragraphs and sentences again and again until the rhythm felt right.

*What is your background in terms of spirituality?*

Both my parents were practicing Christians, and so that was going on in the background for me while I was growing up. But in my teens I began to get disenchanted with the ritualistic side of spirituality, and a more individual, inner enquiry arose in me, fuelled by books such as Richard Bach's *Jonathan Livingstone Seagull* and *Illusions*. Then, in my 20s, I began to look at personal growth from a more psychological perspective, and went on to study Hindu philosophy (Advaita Vedanta) and, later, shaman healing originating from Peru. Of course, at college, learning Chinese medicine, there were forays into Zen and Taoism too. All in all, quite a mixture from all over the world.

*Why do you think the novel is a good form for approaching spiritual ideas?*

As a conveyor of meaning, myth and story have been the means for millennia – from the campfires of our ancestors to the novels of today – which for spiritual ideas can be as air is to music, conveying the essence of something altogether rather wonderful. I came across a great G.K. Chesterton quote recently: "Humour can get in under the door while seriousness is still fumbling at the handle." Like humour, a story can have the same ability to penetrate past our rational, reasoning mind and reach a place where belief is suspended in the service of entertainment. It's here the magic of Truth and Love and Spirit can go to work and provide us with the uplift to soar to new heavens within our being.

*Did the dynamic between the characters have any basis in your own experience? Was there a Wode to your younger self?*

This may sound a bit strange, but despite not having any children there's still a "father" within me and it was this that I often felt coming through while I was writing *Smiling the Moon*. I was both parts of the relationship – the inner boy looking for guidance in life, and also the fatherly teacher, imparting wisdom to nurture the boy's yearning. We all have this duality in some form – our own inner guide and wisdom, and our everyday self – which some call our higher and lower self.

It would have been wonderful to have had a Wode-like figure in my early life, but instead I simply took the wisdom that came through others I met, and from books and courses. But for me the greatest Wode-like influence in my life has been a spiritual teacher called Barry Long. He imparted a modern teaching that is down-to-earth and practical, yet also managed to clearly explain some of the deepest mysteries of the universe; I've found it invaluable.

*Was there any specific inspiration you had in mind when you were writing the book? Either a spiritual text or a novel, or more broadly an idea you wanted to convey at the heart of the book?*

Yes, the whole book is really about karma. From what I can see in the world it's a hugely misunderstood reality, and the closest we get to it in the West is referring to it as fate or destiny, or through the understanding of the old saying, "as you sow, so shall you reap." But it's also about responsibility. If you consider the fact that the state of the world today is a direct result of all humanity's thinking (every war that's ever been is the result of someone thinking it a good idea!), it really brings home how important something as intangible as a thought is to our individual karma, and that of humanity's. On a personal level we instinctively know this is true, for what we acknowledge, we get. So if we are in the habit of focusing on the negative in our lives, that thinking simply attracts more negativity to us.

This, of course, is something Louise Hay highlighted almost 30 years ago.

*Did you learn anything from writing the book?*

It's a cliché, but it really has been quite a journey. Much of it has been spent learning how to adequately capture the essence of an idea within me, and to release it onto the page in a way that can later fly into the reader's mind to be savoured and understood. I've been shown something of the mechanics of storytelling and I sense there are vast depths I've yet to plumb. And I could be deluding myself, but there feels to be a musicality, a rhythm, that can be experienced within prose, which can be enhanced with the right word or punctuation. Above all, I've found a part of myself I didn't really know before, and I've enjoyed opening it up, peeling back the layers and exploring what lies underneath.

*What tips would you give to writers who are facing the challenge of finishing their first novel?*

I was very new to writing when I sat down and began *Smiling the Moon*, and I've learnt an enormous amount along the way. For me the most important thing is to have someone whom you love and trust to believe in what you're writing. While I was courting my wife, who lived in Barcelona at the time, I tentatively emailed her the first few chapters of the book to read. The next day she emailed to say that she had loved reading them, and asked me to send the rest. Well, that for me was the sunshine wind that blew the clouds of doubt away, and with her encouragement my writing flowed like never before.

Have support. Unless you're used to writing and are confident in what comes onto the page, have someone support you with positive endorsements. Show your work to people you trust, and listen to what they say – I found the feedback from friends really helpful and my wife's comments immeasurably so.

Tap into your uniqueness. Perhaps you're influenced by a writer or certain novels you've read – it's hard not to be – but the more you can find your uniqueness, the easier it will be to hit your stride all the way to the end of your book.

Do it for the fun. Even if you're at your favourite table in a bustling café, you're still alone in your thoughts and imagination. Writing therefore has to be something you love and enjoy, otherwise it's an uphill battle or could be a sign that something from your past is blocking your creativity.

Do it for others. The more you aim your writing with the idea of helping people or bringing them pleasure and enjoyment, the more Life will support your endeavour. This was mentioned at the Hay House Writer's Workshop I attended, and it inspired me to work hard to find the best book inside me for the benefit of others.

Not every day is a writing day. On some days writing is impossible, and that's as Life intends it. So if your usual *joie de livres* has left the building, you might as well too!

*How did your interest in writing originate?*

I think it's always been there really, but now that I'm older – like a fine wine improving with age – I might now have something worth saying…

## Acknowledgements

I am eternally grateful for all those that karma brings to light and lighten my path, especially the genius that came through Barry Long; for the love that flows from Maria; the serendipity that is Jennifer Day; the light in John Dickson; the love of words in Mary Tomlinson; and the moresight in Duncan Carson and Michelle Pilley at Hay House.

And the spirit in you that whispers your path just beyond hearing.

# JOIN THE HAY HOUSE FAMILY

As the leading self-help, mind, body and spirit publisher in the UK, we'd like to welcome you to our family so that you can enjoy all the benefits our website has to offer.

 **EXTRACTS** from a selection of your favourite author titles

 **COMPETITIONS, PRIZES & SPECIAL OFFERS** Win extracts, money off, downloads and so much more

 **LISTEN** to a range of radio interviews and our latest audio publications

 **CELEBRATE YOUR BIRTHDAY** An inspiring gift will be sent your way

 **LATEST NEWS** Keep up with the latest news from and about our authors

 **ATTEND OUR AUTHOR EVENTS** Be the first to hear about our author events

 **iPHONE APPS** Download your favourite app for your iPhone

 **HAY HOUSE INFORMATION** Ask us anything; all enquiries answered

## join us online at **www.hayhouse.co.uk**

 Astley House, 33 Notting Hill Gate
London, W11 3JQ
T: 020 3675 2450 E: info@hayhouse.co.uk

# ABOUT THE AUTHOR

**Thomas Lawrence** lives in Edinburgh with his wife, Maria, having moved to the city after running his own health centre in the Scottish Highlands for several years. He fits his writing around his practice as an acupuncturist, cognitive hypnotherapist, herbalist and life coach.

Before devoting his life to helping others through his work, his search for the 'right' job took him on a decidedly circuitous career path through information publishing, film and video PR, and television production. During this time he was also investigating the deeper reality of life through spiritual philosophy, driven by a gnostic desire for knowledge to find the Truth within.

Eventually, one morning, he awoke with the realisation that he was to work as a healer with acupuncture, and over the years he has combined other disciplines in order to best help his client patients. Through his practice and writing he is dedicated to helping others increase their wellbeing, and to find a greater meaning in their lives.

www.graceful-change.co.uk